DETROIT PUBLIC LIBRARY

P9-ASH-214

CONELY BRANCH LIBRARY
4600 MARTIN
DETROIT, MI 48210
(313) 224-6461

Fallin' For THE THUG NEXT DOOR

RELEASE DETROIT PUBLIC LIBRARY

A NOVEL BY

MZ. VENOM

DEC

© 2017

Published by Royalty Publishing House
www.royaltypublishinghouse.com

ALL RIGHTS RESERVED

Any unauthorized reprint or use of the material is prohibited. No part of this book may be reproduced or transmitted in any form or by any means, electronic, or mechanical, including photocopying, recording, or by any information storage without express permission by the publisher.

This is an original work of fiction. Names, characters, places and incidents are either products of the author's imagination or are used fictitiously and any resemblance to actual persons, living or dead is entirely coincidental.

Contains explicit language & adult themes suitable for ages 16+

CONELY BRANCH

PLAY-LIST

Jay Park feat. Simon- Metronome

Jay Park feat. Ugly Duck- Ain't No

BTS- Save Me

Jay Park feat. DJ Wegun- On It

Kris WU- Juice

CL- Hello Bitches

Exo- Lucky One

Monsta X- Gone Bad

Jay Park feat. Gray- Drive

BTS- Come Back Home

MOBB- Full House

CL- Lifted

BTS- You Never Walk Alone

Jay Park feat. Yultron, Loco, and Ugly Duck- Boss

BTS- Hold Me Tight

2NE1- MTBD (CL Solo

BTS- Danger

CL- The Baddest Female

Seventeen- Boom Boom

G-Dragon- One of A Kind

Got7- Paradise

Dean feat. Zico- Pour Up

Dok2 feat. Jay Park- Hands Up

Got7- See The Light

Monsta X- Be Quiet

EXO- Can't Bring Me Down

Seventeen- If I

WORDS TO KNOW

Since I don't speak like anyone but myself, it may be difficult for some to follow my slang. These are words, meanings, and abbreviations to know, when reading my book.

PD – *Police Department*

Blowing smoke - *Smoking*

Det.- *Detective*

Dr.- *Doctor*

Silly - *Stupid or dump*

Bangas - *Gang(s)*

Whip - *Car or truck/Vehicle*

Bread – *Money*

Dolo – *Alone or Solo*

Ratchet/Rat-pack – *Ghetto female(s), slut(s) (depending on use of the word.)*

Shottie or Cannon – *Shotgun or large firearm*

Yapping – *Talking*

Ride – *Vehicle (depending on use of the word)*

Fugly – *Fuckin' ugly*

Twelve, po-po, one-time – *Cops or police officers*

PREVIOUSLY

This Is Me

Zya

*L*et me introduce myself for those that don't know me, my name is Jaz'Zyazia Robinson. Yes, my mother really named me Jaz'Zyazia. As I got older, I felt like she was either drunk as fuck when she conceived me, or high as hell when she had me, to give me a name like Jaz'Zyazia. Can you imagine all the jokes my classmates made about my name in middle school and junior high? I went through all types of crazy ass questions like: "*Where your name come from? Is you from Africa with a name like that?*" Because of the bullshit I went through dealing with my name, I didn't make a lot of friends back then.

At least, not until I made it to high school. Anyways, my friends call me Zya. I am a cool, laid back, down-to-earth type of person, with a little attitude problem on the side. I am also caring, loving, and family oriented. I will admit that I'm a little spoiled, being the only child born to my parents, Marsha and Karl Robinson. My parents are currently separated and on the verge of getting a divorce. My father says he just

1

had a change of heart, since he was caught fucking the baldheaded chick at his job. She'll remain nameless, because I don't care for that bitch too much.

Especially since she decided to come in between my parents and break up a happy home. Anyways, I'm 17, but you will never be able to tell how young I really am with this bodacious body I have. I have perky C-cup breast and a medium waist with a flat tummy. You can say I'm a bit of a big girl, but I'm not fat at all. The only fat on my body is the fat sitting in my juicy bubble booty and thick thighs. I have long black hair touching the middle of my back that I keep styled nicely, thanks to my father providing me with the funds to do so.

My golden-caramel complexion brings out my greyish-green eyes. My kissable, sexy, plump lips seem to draw the attention of all the young hustlers in my neighborhood, but I pay them no mind at all. I got my eyes set on this one guy—my neighbor, Markel Spencer. He's a few years older, lives alone, and drives a Benz truck. I don't know the year and the make, I just know it's black with red and black interior. I haven't necessarily seen it close-up, just from a distance. But all I can say is, his truck is straight fiyah.

I'm not sure what he does for work, I just know Markel got money, and he's fine as hell. My bestie Kitanya, a.k.a. KiKi, be telling me to stop fantasizing about a nigga that's too old for me. But I don't be tryna hear the shit she be talking about. Millian, my other bestie and right-hand bitch, agrees with me sometimes, but she agrees more with Kitanya; she thinks I should let go of wanting to get with Markel too.

She doesn't think we're on the same level, and she's always saying,

"Zya, that nigga may look like he got his shit together and have it all, but he looks like trouble. Besides that, he got too many bitches, and I don't think you should attempt to compete with them for him. You're just too young for him." I let that shit go in one ear and out the other. Like damn, let me do me.

Millian and Kitanya are my girls, but damn, mind your business sometimes. Millian and KiKi got boyfriends, I don't, so why not let me do me, and they could worry about their own niggas. I'm just saying, I'm tired of being lonely and a virgin. I want a nigga to break me off every now and again. They don't have to worry about being alone since they're always with their boyfriends these days. Anyways, Markel is six-feet even, he has these sexy light brown eyes and full lips. He has tattoos all over his muscular chest, back, and arms, covering his caramel complexion, and he sports a low-cut with waves.

Every time I see this man, I feel my heart flutter. I was trying to figure out if I was lusting over this nigga, or if I'd fallen head over heels for this man. Markel and I haven't really said much to each other, except *hi* or *bye* as we passed each other in the streets. I swear, each time we pass each other, I imagine him grabbing me then ripping my clothes off and fucking me on top of his truck. I know, I know, it'll never happen like that, but you can't knock me for fantasizing about it. My mother, Marsha, was downstairs in the kitchen cooking dinner, and I was up in my room listening to music while rocking my hips back and forth.

I was attempting to straighten up my room, so my mother could stop complaining every time she walked up in here without ever knocking on my door, with her rude ass.

They don't ever see you like— I do. First thing, when you wake up. Before you put on your makeup. And they don't really know you like—I do. Cause with me you ain't the same. You ain't gotta run no game. Girl, 'cause what you do and what I do ain't different. We both on a mission, I love your ambition.

And, I know how it is to hit the block and get the gwop. And, you know what it is to hit the stage and make it pop. Like, damn I hope somebody spend some money today. And I pray nobody come and try to take it away. 'Cause I'm just out here doing what I gotta do. 'Cause all these fucking bills are due. And I see all this money to make. So, girl you know that I ain't judging you.

Go and get ya' money, go and get ya' money, go and get ya' money. Baby, I salute. Go and get ya' money, go and get ya' money, go and get ya' money. Make that money girl, it's yours. Spend that money girl, it's yours. You work hard for all of it, it's yours. Work that body baby, it's yours. I ain't judging you. Go and get ya' money, go and get ya' money, go and get ya' money…

I sang with August as his voice blared through the surround sound speakers around my room. A cool breeze blew through the open window, and the curtains swayed from side to side as the wind came through my window. If anyone outside was paying me any attention, all they would see is me rocking to the music while singing with August, as I made my bed then picked up a few pieces of crumbled up paper off the floor. I tossed the paper in the small wicker trash basket over by my desk, which was in front of one out of three windows in my bedroom.

When I was finally done cleaning my room, I sat down at my desk in front of my window just in time to see Markel pull up. Since the only available parking space was directly in front of my house, he had no choice but to park there.

As bad as I wanted to get up and run downstairs and out onto the porch, so he could peep me in my booty shorts and tank top—I didn't. After Markel parked his truck and got out, he walked around to the passenger side of his truck and opened the door. I was disappointed when I saw a female getting out the truck. In fact, I was disgusted at seeing this broad step out his truck, especially dressed the way she was. She had on a pair of tight booty shorts, that showed her camel-toe a little too much, and a shirt that looked like it was a full t-shirt at some point. It was like, she cut it down to resemble a tube top with spaghetti straps or some shit.

Just know, they didn't sell that weird ass looking top in any store that I've been in. That's how I know the dummy had to have made it herself. She was rocking a pair of black pumps with her weird ass outfit, thinking she was cute and wasn't. I heard my mother calling me to come downstairs over the music. If I could hear my mother over the loud music, then you know my mother had a big ass mouth. I sucked my teeth as I got up from the chair, then cut my music off and made my way downstairs to see what my mother wanted.

When I got downstairs, my father was standing beside her. I was thinking to myself, *what the fuck is he doing here, and on a Thursday of all days.*

"Hey Daddy, what's up? It's not Friday, and I don't go to your house this week, I go next weekend. So, what you doin' here?"

"I know, baby, I came to talk to you about something."

"Is it important? I was kind of in the middle of something important myself," I lied.

"Yes, it is… Your mom invited me over for dinner, so we could all talk about it. So, let's go in the dining room and have a seat. Your mom has already set the table."

We all walked in the dining room and sat down at the table. My mom had made mashed potatoes with gravy, fried boneless chicken breast, and corn and string beans on the side. This is what we always ate on Thursdays. Even though I loved fried chicken and potatoes, I didn't like eating the shit every week. My mother had a specific meal she made every day of the week, and yes, she made that same meal every week on that day. I wish she switched it up a little, but this was her routine ever since her and my father parted ways. I didn't complain; I enjoyed each meal my mother cooked in this house.

I tried my best not to give my mother a hard time, because she was having a hard enough time trying cope with her break up from my father. In a way, I was disappointed in my mother for allowing my father to practically get away with cheating on her. She should've beat the shit out of him and the baldheaded bitch at his job. Slash his tires, give that bitch a buck50 across her face—something other than sitting in the house cleaning obsessively and cooking the same shit every week. She thinks I don't know she be up late nights crying over his ass. I love my father to death, but I love my mother too.

I'm a young lady and I stand behind my mother 2,000 percent. I don't ever want to go through the type of pain she's going through over no man. They've been together since freshman year in high school. With all those years of building and taking care of each other, I know my mother's heart done turned into a pile of dust in her chest. I can't even say her heart is shattered into a million little pieces; that shit turned into dust. I felt bad for both my parents, but my heart went out to my mother.

I was hurt too, because my parents were no longer together, and I always thought they would be together forever; I was wrong. When we sat at the table, no one said anything, so I started eating the food my mother had placed in front of me. Today, the fried chicken breast had more flavor to it. The shit was good as hell; I was placing two more pieces on my plate.

"Jaz'Zyazia, slow down child! You didn't even get past the first one; put those two pieces back."

"C'mon Ma, leave me woman. I know what I'm doin'."

"Greedy ass…" she mumbled. I didn't say anything; I just smiled.

"So, Zya, how are you doing in school?" my father asked. I was about to put a forkful of corn and potatoes in my mouth, when my father had asked me that odd ass question about school.

"Daddy, you never ask me anything about school… So, what's up? What's on your mind? Because it seems like you got something to say."

"You have… Have something to say," my mother corrected me. I just looked at her as if she were crazy, over there tryna correct somebody. I gazed back over at my father as I waited for him to speak.

He cleared his throat then said, "Ok, well I wanted to let you know that I'm moving."

"Moving? Where to? You moving to the other side of town, the next city over?"

"No, baby; I'm moving to California, and I wanted to know if you'd like to come with me…"

"Wait—what?"

"I'm—" I cut him off.

"I heard what you said Daddy, damn!"

"Watch your language, Jaz'Zya!"

"Leave her Marsha; it's clear that she's upset about this."

"I don't blame her! How are you going to just walk out of our lives and then come around to try and take her away from me, because you've decided to move clear across the globe to California with your bitch! Who do you think you are?" I sat there watching my parents argue with tears running down my face.

I can't believe my father would just up and move all the way to California like that. Why would he do something like that to begin with, without speaking to me about it before he made his decision to leave? I already see it; he's on some selfish shit. He's thinking of no one but himself, and that's fucked up.

"Don't get mad at me because I left you, Marsha! Get over it, we're done. This isn't about you!" I banged my fork on the table, while looking at my father.

"Then who the hell is it about then, Daddy? You didn't just leave Mommy behind when you decided to cheat on your marriage and walk out! You left me too! Not one time did you think about how I would feel if you two got a divorce, or if you decided to cheat and leave... Not one time! Now suddenly, you feel I should go with you to Cali... Fuck that shit! I'm not going anywhere with you and a bitch you decided to turn your back on your family for! You and that bitch could drop dead!"

I got up from the table and ran out the front door, upset and crying my eyes out. As I ran out the door, I could hear my mother calling out to me. "Zyazia, wait! Zya!" The front door slammed closed as I made my way to the bottom of the steps and out the yard.

I could hardly see through the tears that were running down my cheeks and clouding my vision. I ran smack dead into someone, which knocked me off balance. I felt myself falling backwards towards the ground, until a hand grabbed my arm, then a muscular arm wrapped around my waist.

"You alright?" I heard a deep, manly voice say.

I wiped my eyes and looked up into his handsome face. Staring back at me were a set of light brown eyes that had me mesmerized.

"I-I'm alright... I apologize for running into you like that, I didn't even see you there." I can't believe he had me stuttering like this.

"Is everything ok, why you crying?"

"It's nothing, I need to go." I broke away from his embrace and started walking; that's when I heard his voice call out to me.

"Zya... That's your name right, Zya?" I turned around to face him again. I was shocked that he even knew my name, but I couldn't show it.

"Yeah, that's my name. How do you know my name?"

"We're neighbors and I be hearing your friends calling your name all the time. Besides, it's a catchy name, how could I forget it?"

He smiled this bright, white smile that seemed to pull me in.

"Listen, if you want to come over and talk about what got you crying like that, I'm here for you. I'm good at listening and being the shoulder to lean on when needed."

"Don't you have company already?" *Did I just say that?* "I mean, I don't want to intrude…"

He laughed, "Nah, I don't have company. C'mon, you could be my company. I rather you come talk to me than running these streets in the darkness with your emotions on your sleeves."

"I looked up in the sky and said, "It's not dark…"

"The sun is setting, so it'll be dark soon, and I don't think you want to be out in these streets alone at night."

"Ok, fine. I'll take you up on your offer." I walked with Markel to his house, which was right next door to mine.

He lived on the second floor in a two-bedroom apartment. It was spacious and decorated nicely. We were standing in the living room by the door.

"You can have a seat. Would you like anything to drink? I got soda, bottled water, strawberry kool-aid, and Henny."

"No thank you, I'm good."

"Aight, give me a second, I'll be right back." Markel disappeared to the back of the house for about five minutes, then came back, wearing a wife-beater, a pair of sweat pants, and socks. He sat on the sofa next to me, "So what's up, what's wrong with you? What had you crying and damn near knocking me down?"

"I doubt that I'm close to being strong enough to knock you down. If I'm not mistaken, I was the only one on my way down to the ground."

"Good thing I saved your life."

"Yeah, ok. But thanks anyways."

I shook my head and laughed, because he was too funny. My life wasn't in danger; it was more like he saved me from busting my ass and causing myself to be embarrassed in front of him and everyone else that was outside. "So, what's up? Tell me what happened; maybe I could help you out."

"Well, my parents are getting divorced, and my father has decided to move to Cali with his side bitch."

"Are you and your dad close?"

"We used to be, before him and my mom separated. Now, it's a little different with us. I guess cuz I don't care to be around his bitch. So, our relationship is slowly fading."

"So, if that's the case, then why is you feeling some type of way about him moving to Cali?"

"Because, I won't be able to see him when I want anymore. Just because we're not as close as we used to be, doesn't mean that I hate him completely and want no type of relationship with him. I just don't want to be around the other chick."

"Does he not come around you on his own?"

"I stay with him every other weekend, but we used to see each other a lot in between time. We used to do Daddy-daughter dinner dates, movies, bowling— shit like that. But now, shit's different. He stopped coming around as often, and most weekends with him, I skip out on. He's always tryna get me to spend time with her, but I'm not having that. Just now, after stating that he's moving to Cali, he told me that he wants me to go with him."

"And you don't want to jump on the opportunity of moving to California, right?"

"Nope, I don't. I'm not moving to Cali with her; even if it wasn't her… I'm not leaving my mother behind so we could live it up in Cali without her."

"I feel you, if my mom was still alive and I was put in that same position, I would turn up on my father and make him feel stupid about himself, not saying that you should do that."

"Too late, I went off on him and stormed out the house."

"I don't think you should've ran out, you should've stood your ground and faced him head on. As his kid, better yet, being your own person and having your own identity, you have the right to express how you feel to anybody. Especially your parents. And if they don't understand, or don't want to try to understand, how you feel about the situation, that's on them. Feel me?"

After talking about my issues with my parents to Markel, he decided to flip the conversation to another subject—him. "So, you were watching me earlier?"

"Huh? No, I wasn't watching you. I was looking out my window and you just so happened to pull up and park in front of my house; that's all. That don't mean, I was watching you."

Markel smiled, "It doesn't change the fact that you were watching me, though."

I looked at him like he was crazy, "Negro, wasn't nobody watching you!"

"Yeah, aight. How'd you know I had company, if you weren't watching me?"

"It was obvious; you got out your truck with a ratchet. It wasn't like she lives on this block for you to give her a ride and just drop her off in front of your place and keep it pushing. She was around for one purpose, and it wasn't for a ride, at least not to ride in your truck," I said with a little more attitude than I wanted to express.

"Woah—wait a minute, what's with the attitude? Seems like you mad, why? You like me or something?" Again, he smiled as he looked in my direction.

"*NO!* Why would I like you for, cuz we're neighbors? I think not."

I rolled my eyes and quickly turned my head in the opposite direction to avoid his gaze. I felt my face getting warm. I was blushing off the thought of liking this nigga and him liking me back. But Markel is six years older than me. Why in the hell would he like me—a virgin— when he could have all those other fast tail females that are ready and willing to drop their draws when told to do so?

We talked for another three and a half hours. I looked down at my watch and saw that it was getting late, and I had to get up and take my ass to school early in the morning. Besides, I knew my mother was probably up waiting for me to walk back in the house, so she could go off on my ass.

"I gotta go; it's getting late, and I got school in the morning."

"Oh aight, my bad. What time you leave for school in the morning?"

"Around 6:45; I take a bus to school."

"What school you go to?"

"Bullard Haven."

"Oh, aight. Let me walk you out."

Markel walked me downstairs to the porch and watched me as I walked the short distance to my front door. When I made it to my door, I waved to him then disappeared into the house, leaving him standing on his front porch. I locked the door, then attempted to walk towards the stairs heading for my room, but was quickly stopped in my tracks.

"Jaz'Zyazia Chanel Robinson, bring your black ass in this damn living room!"

My mother's voice echoed through the house. I slowly made my way into the living room, only to see that my father was still here. In a big way, I was kind of disappointed to see him sitting on the sofa like this was still his home. He needed to go to where he belonged, and that was in his own home, where that ugly ass, baldheaded, monkey looking bitch was waiting for him.

"Yes..." I said in a flat tone.

"Where were you all this time?" my father asked.

"Nowhere..." I blurted out, purposely showing him nothing but attitude.

"Zya, what's up with this disrespectful shit you're giving me?" He stood to his feet and walked over and stood in front of me. "Just 'cause you're 17 going on 18, don't mean you're grown enough to talk back and be disrespectful to either one of us. You'll still get that ass whipped up and down this house like you were 12."

"Understood, now can I go to bed? I have school in the morning."

"Zyazia, cut it out and have a seat." My mother spoke, in a soft tone. I did as she told me to do; I walked around my father's 5-foot-11 muscular frame and sat in the chair by the sofa. Not once did I look up in my father's face. I continued to look past him as if he weren't really standing in the room. "Zya, your father wants to spend some time with you over break, before he leaves for California."

"No thank you. I already have plans made for spring break; can't do it."

My father, Karl, turned to face me. "Are your friends more important than spending time with your father? Zya, I'm leaving for California in a couple weeks. I would like to spend these last few weeks with you, if you don't mind."

"Well Karl, I mind... I sure do, and yes, my friends are way more important than a man that decided to abandon his wife and teenage daughter. Sorry to disappoint you, but you've been disappointing me for a while now. So, I guess it's only fair."

My words must've stabbed him deeply in his heart, because he rushed over to me and slapped the spit out of me, causing my head to fling to the side.

"I'm tired of this disrespect coming from you! I'm tired!" I grabbed my face as my mother stood to her feet.

"What the hell is wrong with you, Karl?! Don't be putting your damn hands on her like that! Have you lost your fuckin' mind?!"

My father's face went from being pissed off to hurt, when he saw the look of surprise on my face as tears were streaming silently from my eyes.

"Zya, I—"

My mother cut in, "You nothing—it's time for you to go! Get out, now. This conversation shouldn't've ever happened. Go!"

Before my father could move, I jumped up out the chair and darted up the stairs to my bedroom and slammed my door shut. I wanted to turn into a savage and destroy my room, but then cleaning it earlier would've been a waste of my time. I chose to lay my ass in my bed and cry myself to sleep instead. I cried until I couldn't cry anymore. Hours had passed me by, yet my parents were still downstairs arguing. My father yelled about how he didn't mean to hit me, but I had provoked him into doing so.

My mother retaliated by telling him, she wasn't allowing me to go all the way to California with him. That's when he finally got mad enough to leave, slamming the door behind as he left. I couldn't sleep to save my life, so I lay in my bed looking up at the ceiling, thinking about Markel and the conversation we had. I couldn't believe I was in his house conversing with him. Hell, I was surprised that he even took the time to converse with me to begin with. I wonder if he's still up or is he sleeping, like my ass should be.

I wonder if I tell him that I have this crazy crush on him, will he tell me he likes me too? Yeah right; like Kitanya keeps saying, that nigga is not worried about my young ass. He has other bitches he deals with. Fuck all that; I bet I can make him forget all about them chicks. They're not worth his time, anyways. But then again, I don't really think I'm worth his time either. What the hell would he want with me, a young virgin? I have nothing to offer him but a pretty smile and good conversation.

CHAPTER 2

I Can't Believe It

Zya

The next day

*D*on't ask me when I finally dosed off last night, because I can't even remember. But here I am, rushing to get dressed and brush my teeth. After sliding my feet into black and pink Jordans to match the black and pink outfit I had on, I ran a big tooth comb through my hair to lay it down. I was running a couple minutes late and didn't want to miss my bus. I grabbed a hair tie and wrapped it around my wrist, then snatched my varsity jacket and my bookbag off the chair, and then rushed out my room and downstairs.

"Zyazia, I made breakfast for you!" my mother yelled from the kitchen.

"Sorry Mom, I'm running late. I'll warm it up, when I get home."

"You can't warm grits up and think it'll taste good later. I'll have something fixed for you when you get out of school. Don't forget, I work overnight tonight at the hospital. I'll leave some money on the counter for you before I leave out."

"Alright, I'm going now."

"Love you, baby."

"Love you too, Mommy."

I rushed out the door before she could say anything else. When I closed the door and rushed down the stairs, I noticed Markel was leaning up against his truck like he was waiting for somebody. I was confused at why he was just standing there, especially this early in the morning. The only ones up now, were people on their way to work and high school students tryna make sure they didn't miss their bus—like me. I walked out the gate as I looked him dead in his face. I was curious to know what his reason was for standing there looking like a fool so early in the morning.

"Good morning, neighbor," I said to him.

"Yeah, it is—isn't it?" Markel replied.

"What're you doing out here so early in the morning?"

"Got up to take you to school."

"Huh? Why would you do that?"

"You're too pretty to be catching a school bus; them things are too noisy, anyways. C'mon, get in."

Markel opened the passenger side door. At first, I hesitated to get in. But then, I thought about how early in the morning it was and realized he could've still been in bed sleeping. But here he was, out here in the cold morning air to take me to school. I didn't have to think about it any longer; I got in the truck, allowing Markel to close the door. He walked around to the driver side and got in.

Not long after, we were pulling up the block. I can't believe my neighbor, Markel Spencer, the guy I've had a crush on since I was 13-years old, is giving me a ride to school. I could feel my heart beating fast; I was excited. People were about to see me in this dope ass truck with Markel. Now that I think about it, I was alone with Markel. Not only was I alone with Markel, but he was driving me to school.

Oh my gosh, I'm so nervous. What should I say to him? Wait— wait a second, Zya... You were alone with this nigga last night, and y'all conversed for a few hours with no one else around. What the fuck is you nervous for? He's just giving you a ride to school, so stop buggin', girl, I thought to myself.

I was tripping for nothing; it was just a ride. It wasn't like we were going somewhere private to get our freak on. I had to take a couple deep breaths and exhale as I turned to look out the window. We were just about to get off the highway, when Markel decided to speak to me first.

"You good? You real quiet over there."

"Yeah, I'm good, just amazed you got up hella early in the morning to take me to school."

"We're neighbors, why wouldn't I offer you a ride to school?"

"Oh, so you always get up at 6:45 in the morning to give your neighbors rides to school?"

"Nah, but—."

"Negro, please… We've been neighbors since I was 13. It took you five years to speak to me, besides saying hi or bye, and now you've graduated to giving me rides. Why?"

"Like I said, you're too pretty to be getting on some loud school bus with a bunch of annoying kids."

"I think, you're full of shit. But thanks for the ride anyways, I do appreciate it."

"Let me be full of shit, then," he said with a smile on his face.

Fifteen minutes later, we'd pulled up to my school. Markel parked outside the gate, and I started to get out, until he gently grabbed my wrist. I looked back at him, "What's up?"

"What time you get out of school?" he asked.

"At 2:40, I think… I'm not sure if we get out early or not today. Why you wanna know for?"

"I'll be out here to pick you up. I wanna take you somewhere wit' me later. I mean, if you good wit' that."

"Um, yeah, I guess…"

"You gotta phone?"

"Yeah…"

"Let me see it."

I dug in my pocket, pulled out my phone, then handed it to Markel. I watched him put his number in my contacts, then he handed my phone back.

"Find out what time you get out, then text me."

"Ok, I'll do that."

"See you after school."

"Later."

I got out and made my way inside the gate and towards the building, where I spotted Kitanya and Millian waiting for me. As I approached Kitanya and Millian, KiKi looks over at me with this crazy look on her face.

"Ah uh bitch, who's truck did you just get out of? You think we didn't peep that shit, but we did. Who was that?"

"None of ya' business, damn nosy! C'mon, we gonna be late for first period."

"Nah, fuck first period! I wanna know who that was, or I'm gonna make ya' ass late on purpose." I looked at Kitanya as we walked in the building and into the crowded hallways.

"Don't say no ill shit if I tell you who it was. I don't need to be hearing no shit from you. I already been through enough with my father last night."

"Whaa? Your father? What happened with your father?" Millian asked.

"The jerk slapped the shit outta me, because I spoke the truth to his ass."

Millian's head swung in my direction, "Are you serious? You alright?"

"I'm standing here right now, ain't I?"

"Girl, you probably deserved it. Don't be getting smart, lizard face."

"Alright, don't start with the name calling, dick nose." Millian and I laughed in unison.

"That was a good one, '*dick nose*'... I'm gonna call my mother that shit when she gets on my nerves with all her foolery."

"Don't do that, stupid! I would punch you in your neck myself."

"Whatever," she replied.

Kitanya interrupted, "Uh, HELLO! You just gonna ignore my question? Who the hell was in the truck, wit' ya' secretive ass?"

"It was Markel, ok. Damn, you so fuckin' nosy!"

"*MARKEL*?" Kitanya and Millian both said at the same time.

"Yes, Markel! He wanted to give me a ride to school, so I let him. And, he's picking me up after school."

"Wait a minute, you talkin' 'bout the same nigga you said you've lived next door to all this time, that you've been crushing on since you were younger? Bitch, let that nigga alone and move the fuck on wit' ya' life," Kitanya said as we walked to our lockers.

We made it to our lockers, which were across the hall from each other. That was the only time we had a quiet moment between us, because I wasn't into yelling across the hallway at one another. I grabbed my books for the first three periods, which were algebra, biology, and African American History. After that, I had a free period, which is called study hall, and then lunch. I predicted this day was going to pass by pretty fast. Once I closed my locker, me and my girls took our asses to class, arguing about Markel, once again.

Kitanya, Millian, and I had damn near all the same classes together, except our trade classes. How the hell did that happen, right? I guess it was pure luck that I had almost all the same classes with these two crazy mamas. Millian took hairdressing, Kitanya took auto, and I was in bakery, only 'cause I didn't want to take culinary arts with all that extra shit they had to do. I love to cook; I've always wanted to be head chef in my own restaurant. Four long years of taking up bakery helped me a lot; it brought me a few steps closer to doing what I wanted to do.

Well, not really, but I was good with taking that class, since I always ace every test and my food be banging. After the first two classes, the day seemed to zip on by without a hitch. After third period, I heard from the teacher that we were getting out early today. For me, that meant lunch, free period, then home. That wasn't a problem for me. I texted Markel during lunch to let him know we were getting out around twelve today. Kitanya and Millian wanted to get up after school and chill, but I declined after reminding them I already had plans. KiKi was giving me the side-eye.

"Why not, what're you doin' after school?"

"I have somewhere to go. I already told both of you this earlier. Why are you tryna be up in my business, though?"

"Bitch, you don't have any business to be in. All you do is come to school and go straight home afterwards, like a good little girl," she said. I could still hear attitude in her voice, like she was really mad that I was going with Markel after school.

"Not today and you mad about it." I giggled.

Millian jumped in, "Kitanya, mind your damn business for a change. I don't recall Zya being your daughter."

"I'm happy she ain't, or I'd put my foot so far up her ass, that she'll be shitting leather for a year."

"Whateva, bitch, that'll never happen." I looked down at my phone as the loud ass, annoying bell rang.

We headed for study hall in the library. This was the only time I planned to focus on any school work. Once I leave this building, I won't be picking up another school book until the weekend before we come back. I wasn't about to spend my entire week studying for a test that I already knew I would pass. I was ready to enjoy my week off from school. Hopefully, I won't have to see my father's face, because I was hoping for a drama free week. With him around, there would be nothing but drama, and I didn't need that. Almost 30 minutes later, the bell sounded off for the last time, letting us know school was a wrap.

We got up and made our way to our lockers. Today was the start of our week-long spring break. I was mad we were told to study for a test in African American History, as much as I didn't want to study nothing but Markel's muscular body and handsome smile. I knew I was fooling myself. I placed my biology and math books in my locker and grabbed two notebooks that held my notes from last week's history exam. After placing my notebooks in my bookbag, I closed my locker and made my way out of the building with Millian and Kitanya by my side.

We walked towards the gate, talking about what we had planned for the weekend and the week we had off from school. Soon as we made it to the gate, I heard music playing loud, catching the attention of mostly everyone that walked out the gate. I heard a horn beep twice, catching my attention as well as Millian and Kitanya's. We turned in the direction of the horn, only to see Markel's sexy ass looking in our direction with a smile on his face.

"Excuse me ladies, I'll be right back."

Kitanya said, "Is that him? Is that the infamous, Markel?"

"Yes, it is."

"Go handle ya' business," Kitanya said with attitude in her tone.

I looked at her and rolled my eyes as I walked over to the truck. Markel was bumping my favorite boy toy, August Alsina, loud enough for the entire school to hear through windows that were rolled down halfway. When I walked over and stood by the car, he turned the music down and rolled the window all the way down.

"What's good, those your friends?"

"Yeah, they are."

"They need a ride? Tell them to c'mon; I'll give them a ride."

"You don't have to do that, Markel. You don't even know them…"

"They're your friends, so it doesn't matter."

"Alright, fine."

I called Kitanya and Millian over, then got in the truck.

Once we all were in, I introduced Kitanya and Millian to Markel, then we pulled away from the curb. As soon as we pulled from the curb, Kitanya starts in on Markel with a bunch of questions.

"So, Markel, what do you do to get money? Because this truck looks like it cost a lot. Not to mention that Rolex on your wrist; you smell like new money." Markel looked over at me as I looked back at Kitanya.

"KiKi, is you serious right now?"

"I'm just asking, since this nigga rolling up to the school to get you like he ya' man and offering rides and whatnot. I just wanna make sure we not gonna get pulled over and locked the fuck up at some point."

"It was your choice to get in this bitch, so stop fussing over nothing."

"And? That's not the point."

"There is no point, not coming from you. You need to chill the fuck out!" I turned back in my seat; I couldn't even look at Markel.

I was embarrassed by Kitanya's hating ass. Millian didn't say anything, she just looked over at Kitanya shaking her head from side to side. Markel said nothing; he continued to drive quietly as I directed him to KiKi's house. She was the first beast that was getting dropped the fuck off. She had to go before I was forced to reach in the back seat and connect my fist with her lips. I don't know what her problem was, but she definitely overdid it today.

As Markel pulled onto her street, she said, "Good thing we're at my house, huh? Too bad, because I had more questions for you. But I won't forget you didn't answer any of my questions either."

Millian said, "Ki, get the fuck out the truck and shut the hell up," as Markel pulled up to the curb.

As Kitanya got out the truck, Millian continued, "Sorry about that Markel, she can't help herself. Pay her ass no mind, though. I'll get out with this broad; see you later, Zya."

"Later, Millz." Millian got out with Kitanya. We watched them go inside Kitanya's house, before Markel pulled off.

"I apologize for that, Markel." I still couldn't even look at him while speaking to him.

"Don't worry about it, it's nothing. What happened after you got in the house last night?" I looked over at Markel shaking my head.

"Please, don't even ask. I walked into the gates of hell. My father was still there when I got in. I was hoping he would've been gone, but he wasn't. Things heated up pretty fast and got out of control to the point things got physical."

"You serious? Ya' pops put his hands on you?" I didn't say anything; I just looked out the window thinking about how my father's hand went across my face. "You good?

"Yeah, I'm straight. Things could've been worse than what they were. My mother stepped in. She knew my father was wrong and his actions were uncalled for. He was in the wrong, but he just made my eyes open wide as fuck. He should know I would never move with him, especially after that mess last night."

"Well, fuck dat nigga. Today, we gon' spend the day enjoying ourselves."

"Doing what?" I asked as I finally turned to look in his face.

Markel pulled into the parking lot in front of Showcase Cinema movie theatre. He shut the truck off after finding a parking spot and parking his truck. We sat there for a minute in silence as he rolled a blunt.

"You smoke?"

"Nope."

"Do you mind if I smoke this real quick before we go in?" I peeped him looking at me waiting for my answer.

"No, I don't mind. Go ahead and do you."

He lit one end of the blunt as he put it to his lips, then inhaled the smoke. Once he blew out the smoke, he said, "You got a man?"

"Nope, I don't," I answered back.

"Why not?" he asked.

"Between playing basketball and my girls, I don't have time for a boyfriend."

"Oh, so dating is seasonal to you?"

"What do you mean? Dating isn't a season thing to me; I just don't have time for a boyfriend. Seeing Millian and KiKi and how stressful their relationships are, I don't think it's worth me even getting involved with anybody right now. I'm more worried about prom and graduating this year."

"You a virgin, huh?"

"What? What are you saying, I feel that way because I may be a virgin or something?"

"I'm saying, you sound like you scared to deal with a nigga."

"Are we speaking of a specific person, or are we generally speaking? Cuz you buggin' with your line of questioning."

He blew smoke out his mouth once again. "I'm just asking to ask. If I were asking for a specific person, it would be for me."

"You?"

"Why you say it like that, you wouldn't go out with me?"

"You have way too many females in your little circle. You wouldn't be the man for me, nope."

"I don't think you being real. I know you be watching me out your bedroom window."

"You're thinking too much; I don't be watching you—not at all."

"You're lying, I peeped you watching me the other day, not to mention last Summer when you were sitting on your porch with your friends. You tried hard to pretend like you weren't, but I peeped you watching me."

"Whateva, nigga… You don't know what you're talking about."

"Aight, come here."

With one hand, Markel grabbed my shirt and pulled me close in his space. He moved his face closer to mine. I looked into his chinky looking eyes and said, "What are you doing?" Without responding, Markel connected his lips with mine. At first, he pecked my lips with a kiss, then he kissed me passionately for a few minutes. I'm talking about with tongue and all.

Within that small amount of time, I felt this warm-tingly feeling sweep through my body. I don't know why, or how, but I felt high as fuck off this man. It could've been the weed smoke that had me feeling the way I was feeling, but I highly doubt it. I've always dreamed he would be the one to give me my first kiss and look—my dreams came true. Damn it, Markel why are you doing this to me? He removed his lips from mine, then sat back in his seat. I was stuck in the same spot, leaning over towards him with my eyes closed.

In my head, he was still kissing my lips. He cleared his throat, alerting me that the dream was over.

"Thought you didn't like me?" Markel questioned.

"I don't, you kissed me."

"And you kissed me back. C'mon, the movie is about to start."

He got out the truck, walked around to the passenger side, then opened the door for me. He helped me out the truck, and then closed the door. We started walking towards the street, and that's when I saw him press a button on his keychain securing the locks. We were walking across the street towards the theatre when Markel took my hand and wrapped his hands around mine. I looked down at our hands, then up at his face. He was looking straight ahead as we continued into the building.

CHAPTER 3

Do You Like...

Zya

After the movie

When the movie was over, we headed back to my house. My mother was at work and wouldn't be back until tomorrow morning, so I didn't mind Markel keeping me company. I offered him something to drink, but he declined the offer. So, I told him to have a seat in the living room. I went upstairs to change my clothes, because I still had my uniform on and needed to change into something more comfortable. I came downstairs sporting a pair of black fitted stretchy shorts and a pale pink tank top with matching black and pink ankle socks on my feet. When I walked in the living room, Markel looked up in my direction. His eyes connected with my body. I peeped how his eyes ran down my thick frame and back up to my face.

"Why are you looking at me like that? Close your mouth dummy," I said as I walked over and sat down at the opposite end of the sofa. "Are you hungry? I can order something to eat, if you'd like."

"Nah, I'm good." He licked his lips, while trying to turn his head away, but couldn't. He was now staring in my direction.

"What? Do you have something to say? Because you're staring like you do, and you're making me feel kind of weird… Could you stop?"

"My bad, it's just that you're looking good right now. I never knew you were stacked like that."

"Stacked like what?" I looked down at my body, pretending like I didn't know what he was talking about. In my head I was like, *Yeah nigga, look at this bangin' ass body. I look way better than all those random ass ratchet bitches you've been messing with.*

"You're beautiful, very beautiful, that's all. Any guy would be lucky to have you as their girl."

"Even you?"

"Huh? Thought you didn't like me, why you wanna know?"

"I don't like you, but since you like me so much, I'm just asking." He laughed like I had just told a joke.

"Yeah, even me… You're the type of female that any nigga would wife up. You'll be number one."

"Number one? You say that like you would have a trail of bitches behind me…"

"Why every time you speak about me and other females, you sound like you mad?"

"Huh—um… No, I'm not mad. Why would I be mad if I don't

like your ass? Why you keep saying that I like you, when I already told you that I don't?"

"Cuz, I know you do. I already proved that at the movies, so you can stop frontin'. Ain't nobody around for you to front like that. It's just me and you, so you can be real wit' me."

"I don't…"

"I think you do—no, I know you do. Especially by the way your crazy friend reacted once she met me. Why would she flip on me like that without even knowing who I am? You must talk about a nigga a lot for your friends to react the way they did."

"They? It was only Kitanya. She always acts like that with dudes that approach me or come around me. She's a bit overprotective."

"Nah, she just nosy or jealous."

"Why would she be jealous? I don't go out with you for her to be jealous, and besides, she has a boyfriend."

"Aight, if you say so. We not talkin' 'bout her anyways, we talkin' 'bout you and why you keep frontin' on me. Just say you like me and have always liked me, and I'll make you mine, right now." I looked in his eyes thinking about all the times I've seen him coming and going from his house.

I thought about all the times I wanted him to notice me, and now here he was sitting in my living room. I thought about all the times I fantasized about him kissing me, touching me, and holding me in his arms. I wanted so badly to be with him, but I wasn't going to be the one to admit it first. Nope, I didn't want to look like the desperate neighbor, stalking my crush until he becomes mine. Hell no, I would look crazy as fuck.

"Why don't you admit that you like me, and we can move on with the rest of our day," I said in a bold tone, trying to take charge of the situation.

"I can admit it, can you?"

"Well then, admit it and stop procrastinating."

"Aight fine, Zya. I've been noticed you a while back. I've always thought you were beautiful and always wanted to make you my girl. I like you, and yeah, I do want you to be mine. You satisfied?"

I smiled, "That was whack…"

"Damn, Zya, you mean," he said with a smirk on his face.

I laughed in playful manner, "No sir, I was just playing. Ok—alright, Markel. I'll play ya' game… Yes, I've always noticed you too. I've had a crush on you since I was 13, and I still do. You happy? But I also noticed all the females you're courting, and I'm not feeling that. As much as I like you, I'm not tryna be fighting no bitches over no nigga. That's not how I get down."

"You think if you were my girl, I would still have whatever females you think I have around me? Nah, I'm not that type of dude."

"If you say so…" I looked away for a minute, because in a way, I didn't believe him. But the look he was giving me, said that he was speaking nothing less than the truth. "I'm a virgin…"

"Alright, I already knew that."

"You're the first guy that I've kissed, Markel. And if we get together and go that far, you would be my first…"

He didn't say anything; he just sat there. It looked like he was in deep thought. I was feeling as if I'd turned him off by blurting out that I was a virgin.

"Why are you telling me this like I would turn my back on you and stop liking you cuz you a virgin? That'll just make our bond a little more special than what it is now. Zya, I'll take care of you like a real nigga is supposed to. I won't hurt you, I promise."

I didn't say anything at first, but then the look in his eyes had me caught up in the moment. I moved closer to him on the sofa.

"Markel, every time I look at you, my heart flutters. My body gets warm, and I feel butterflies in my stomach. You make me nervous as hell, but every time I see you with another female, I also get mad as fuck. I don't know what the hell that means… But, if I place my heart in your hands…"

"I won't break your heart, Zya. I won't do dat." Markel cupped my face in his hands and pulled me close. We shared a kiss that had my thighs shaking, my heart melting, and my pussy getting moist, all at the same damn time. He had me on lock; I think that was the very moment I'd fallen head over heels for this nigga. But I wasn't about to tell him that—at least not right now.

We parted lips and I quickly stood to my feet, because I wanted to jump on top of Markel and rip his clothes off. He was making me horny, but I was scared as hell. I've never been penetrated before and wasn't bold enough to allow him inside of me just yet. If we continued like this, I don't know what I'd do.

"You aight?" Markel questioned.

"Ye—yes, I'm alright. I need to take a shower and figure out what I'm gonna do the rest of the day."

It was around four in the afternoon, too early to lie and say I was going to bed. If I'd said that, he would know I was trying to dismiss him or avoid something. But as nervous as I was right now, I'm sure he already knew something was up. His phone started ringing at the right time. He answered on the second ring, but without speaking a word; he ended the call once he was done listening to the voice on the other end. When he looked back at me, he stood to his feet.

"I gotta head out, but I'll be back a little later." He walked over and kissed my lips, then he left.

I just looked from the empty spot on the sofa where'd he sat, then towards the front door that he'd just walked out of, wondering who the hell was that on the other end of his call. How the hell is he just gonna to leave like that? I didn't even tell him to leave yet. Geesh. After all that we just shared with each other, he just left like it was nothing.

"That better not have been one of his bitches that got him running like that," I said out loud to myself.

I walked to the door, locked it, then made my way to the kitchen to see how much money my mother had left for me. When I got to the kitchen, I looked on the island bar and saw money sitting atop a note she'd left for me.

It said:

Jaz'Zya, here's $100. I have to work a double shift and won't be home until late Sunday night. I'm sorry, my love. I'll call home to check in on you whenever I get the chance. Or send me a text and let me know everything *is alright. You can have Millian spend the weekend with you, if you'd like. But, keep Kitanya's grown ass home, where she belongs. Anyways, I love you baby. Call you later.*

Love, Mom

It wasn't that my mother didn't like Kitanya, but she didn't allow her to sleep over my house, because she caught her and her boyfriend Jeff in my front yard making out. The part my mother didn't like was, when they knew she was standing there, they didn't bother to stop. My mother thought it was disrespectful, and so did I. KiKi, apologized to my mother a few days later, but for my mother, her apology wasn't good enough. Her apology was a few days too late. Since then, my mother has always looked at her with that side-eye.

Kitanya seemed to always brush my mother's feelings towards her to the side, but I be tryna remind her that my mother would go upside her head and whip her ass, not caring who her parents are. But, you know KiKi, she thinks she's untouchable. I let her think what she wants, but I don't allow her to bring Jeff around my house anymore. And she knows not to ever disrespect my mother again, because then, she would have to worry about me going upside her head too. My mother aggravates the hell out of me sometimes, but I love her to death and would beat anybody's ass for disrespecting her. KiKi knows she only gets one warning because she's my bestie, but she's lucky she got to slide with just a warning.

You don't get a second time to act out in front of my mother. Anyways, that was months ago. We've moved on from all that and left all that in the past. I took the money my mother left me and went upstairs to my room. I didn't have any plans to go back out the house, so I took out a pair of lime green sweat pants and black tank top out my dresser and sat them on my bed with a fresh pair of underwear and matching bra. I made my way into the bathroom and ran the water in the tub.

I allowed the water to fill the tub as I got undressed. Once the water was filled a little above the halfway point, I cut it off and climbed inside with my washcloth and bar of pink Dove soap in hand. I could feel my clit pulsating, so I reached down in between my thighs. With my middle finger, I started massaging my clit in a circular motion. Instantly, I felt a warm feeling run down my body from head-to-toe. I closed my eyes as I seductively moaned out in a low tone.

The pleasure I felt couldn't be explained. I started moving my hips back and forth, imagining Markel's head between my thighs tasting me, as I started to quickly reach my peak. "Oooow—sshh…" I felt a flood of warm thick fluids cover my finger, as I felt my pussy walls growing tighter as it pulsated. I felt weak and was now ready to take my ass to sleep. I stood from the water and washed my body; when I was done, I rinsed the soap off and let out the water from the tub.

When the tub was empty, I ran the shower. I stepped in the shower and thoroughly washed my body a second time, thinking about Markel the entire time. I rinsed the soap off, got out, and wrapped myself in a towel. Afterwards, I made my way into my room, dried off, and then got dressed. I lay across my bed, then picked up my phone to see that I had two missed calls and four text messages. I had a message from my mother, which I instantly replied to, because she was fussing with me about missing both her calls.

I had messages from Millian and Kitanya. KiKi was still hating on Markel, which I thought it was real corny of her to be doing. Markel was right, it was starting to sound like she was either being nosy or straight jealous. Why was she going so damn hard, when she had her own fucked up ass relationship to worry about? Millian was letting me know that she'd made it home, and had expressed to me how Kitanya was hating on whatever it was that I had going on with Markel. I replied to her text telling her to come to my house in an hour, but without KiKi. I didn't need her type of stress or drama fucking up the rest of my evening.

After reading Markel's text, I replied back to him, letting him know I was about to chill with Millian for a few hours and would get back to him later. That's if he wasn't busy with whoever he ran out my house for earlier. He told me he would hit me up later, when he's finished doing what he's doing. The thing is, I didn't know what he was doing right now. It was all a big mystery to me. I wasn't sure if I should care since I wasn't officially his girlfriend.

Maybe I should mind my business—but then again, the nigga wanted to get with me. So, I wasn't about to mind my business. I planned to ask him about the call he received while at my house, and what he was doing after he left my house. Straight like that, I wasn't about to play no games with him. He was making it easy for me to want to be all up in his business. Was it petty of me to use him wanting to get with me as an excuse to do so? It doesn't matter, cuz I don't care.

CHAPTER 4

A Night Full Of Surprises

Zya

An hour later

$\mathcal{I}$ was just getting off the phone with the pizza place, when I heard the doorbell ring twice. I'd gotten hungry while waiting on Millian to bring her ass on. I loved this chick to death, but she was slower than a freaking goat when it came to getting ready and leaving the house. I got up from the sofa, walked to the front door, and opened it to see Millian standing there with a bag in her hand and a smile on her face.

"What's goodie my homie!" She spread her arms wide as if she was waiting on a hug. I laughed, because she was too funny.

"Girl, bye! Bring ya' ass in this house and close the door with your over excited ass," I playfully said as I walked away from the door and into the living room.

Millian closed the door and made her way into the living room, right behind me. We sat down on the sofa. Millian leaned forward and placed the bag on the table. I looked from Millian to the bag. I already knew she had a bunch of junk food in there, but I still asked what was in it anyways.

"What's not in the bag? Shit, I got everything in there from chips, candy, and soda. Lil' chocolate cakes, donuts; it don't matter, I got it all in the bag like the grocery store." She giggled.

"Greedy ass." I giggled. "But, what do you have in there for me?"

"Child, you know I always bring two of everything when I come here. If I'm getting fat, bitch, so are you."

"Biotch, I'm thicker than a snickers, but I can never get fat."

"You and me both, shit."

"As much as your greedy ass eats, you would think your ass would blow the fuck up."

"Nope, not I. I fuck too much for all that," Millian replied.

"You be fucker-cising a lot, huh?" We busted out laughing as I continued cracking jokes. "You be drinking a lot of protein shakes to help you keep your energy up?"

"Yeah, can't have enough nut-shakes in a day." She laughed.

"Bitch, you nasty." I playfully hit Millian's leg.

Millian is about 5'5 in height, she's white and black mixed, and thick as hell. Yes, my girl is stack liked me in all the right places, with her wide hips, flat belly, thick ass thighs, and round bubble booty. But with her long, reddish brown hair and blueish-grey eyes, make this bitch look scary as hell to some people. But to me, she's beautiful, and

I peep how all the guys in school be trying to holla at her, knowing she got a man. Her nigga goes to Harding High, which is right up the street from our school. As faithful to Vaughn's crazy ass as she is, those niggas be wasting their time trying to get with her.

"All jokes aside, what happened with you and Markel when y'all dropped us off?" Millian questioned.

At first, I was hesitant. I didn't want to tell her anything, because I didn't need another one of my friends catching ill feelings towards me, because someone had finally wanted to get with me. I don't know if Kitanya was more upset about me liking Markel, or the fact that Markel could actually like me back. I was confused at why she always seemed to have an attitude with me, or why she showed out the way she did in front of Markel. The shit was hella disrespectful, not only to me, but to Markel as well. She made herself look crazy though, because the only one that really gave a fuck was her. I really don't care much for her attitude towards me or Markel; she can keep it all to herself.

"Oh, he took me to the movies."

"Wait, so you ditched us to go to the movies with that nigga?"

"Yup, I sure did."

Millian smiled, "Good, because he's fine, and you deserve to go somewhere—shit, anywhere with a fine ass nigga like Markel."

"I thought you and KiKi didn't want me to even bother with Markel..." I looked Millian dead in her eyes.

"First off, it wasn't that I didn't want you to be bothered with him, it was the fact that you liked him for so damn long and hadn't made not one attempt to talk to the man. Yes, I did have a problem with his age,

45

but it's your choice who you like or dislike. I'm not your mother to tell you what to do. Bitch, I'm ya' best friend—ya' muthafuckin' sistah! I'm gonna ride with you no matter what you decide to do. It's your life, so live it the way you see fit."

I smiled, because I could always count on Millz to keep it 5,000 percent real with me all the time. She wasn't the type to smile up in your face like shit was sweet, and talk behind your back later. She always spoke what was on her mind and didn't care about how you felt about her truth. That's why, I loved this bitch to death and beyond.

"Thank you, Millz, I appreciate that a lot."

"Well, since you appreciated my friendship that much, how about you tell me the full story. What happened?"

"We talked before going into the movies and had a moment."

"A moment? What kind of moment?" she questioned.

"He told me how he's been feeling me and been wanting to get with me."

"Well damn, why hasn't he?"

"I don't know, I didn't ask. Anyways, shut up and let me finish."

"My bad, go ahead."

"After he kept trying to get me to confess to him about liking him, he kissed me." Millian's eyes grew wide, as her jaw dropped out of shock. "Yup, the nigga kissed me to see if I was lying, since I kept denying that I liked him. I'll just say that he won the game. We both confessed to each other. After the movies, we came back here and—"

Millian blurted out, "Oh, GOD—you fucked him?"

"Bitch, no! We kissed again, this time it was more meaningful. He made me nervous, because he had my body heating up and shit. I was feeling all these different kinds of emotions; I didn't know what to do. He had to leave, so I was relieved."

"Let me find out this nigga had my girl finger popping in the shower and shit." I looked away out of embarrassment. Not another word came out of my mouth; I couldn't even deny it. "Zya, you serious? That nigga had you going crazy like that?" She tapped my leg with her hand.

"Change the subject; I don't want to talk about this anymore."

Millian started giggling.

"Awe, my baby is ready to become a woman." She playfully pushed my arm once, the second time her hand touched my arm it hurt like hell. She had punched me in the arm, sending a tingling shockwave of pain through it. "You better not, either!"

"Ouch, bitch! That shit doesn't fuckin' tickle! What the hell is wrong with your crazy ass?" I yelled out.

"You better hold out for as long as possible. Tell that nigga you're a virgin and you scared. Tell him you want to wait until you're ready. I don't approve of you losing your innocence right now, or ever!"

"Not too long ago you were telling me that you weren't gonna tell me how to live my life, and that you weren't my mama."

"Well, I changed my mind!"

"Millian, you know you crazy, right?"

A smile crossed her pretty little face. "Yeah, I know," she proudly said. "That's why you keep me around, because of my craziness. I keep you on your toes, bitch."

"Yeah, you do, and you get on my freaking nerves too."

The doorbell rang; I knew it was the pizza delivery guy. So, I gave Millian the money after complaining about my arm being stiff and in pain. She silently shook her head, while taking the money and getting the order from the delivery guy. We ate pizza, watched movies, and conversed until about nine thirty. She helped me clean up our mess, then left after receiving a text message from Vaughn. Now, I was all alone once again. I wasn't tired; I was wide awake and didn't know what to do with myself.

I went outside and sat on my steps, to see Markel's truck wasn't parked out front. He hadn't come home yet, which made me a little curious to know what he was doing. I pulled my phone from my pocket and sent him a text.

Me: Hey wyd?

I didn't receive a text back right away; that shit came almost five minutes later.

Markel: Finishing up something real quick. What up, though?

Me: Nothing, u busy. I'll ttyl, bye.

Markel: Nah, too late. I'm done now. I'm omw to you now.

I wasn't going to respond at first, because for some reason, I was already mad. But, my fingers had a mind of their own.

Me: Nope, stay with the chick you're wit'. I'm off to bed, goodnight.

He didn't respond, that's when I knew I was right. He claimed he was busy, but he was with a ratchet all this time. That was real fucked up of him, especially after what we'd said to each other tonight. Not to mention, the nigga done kissed me a few times. Why was he fucking with my head already? I'm done, before I even got started with his ass. I'm not putting myself through that type of madness.

Just then, Markel pulled up and parked in front of my house.

Damn, I didn't even have time to get my ass up and go in the house. He must've been on his way here the whole time, unless...

Hearing the truck door slam shut, tore me out of my thoughts, as I watched Markel walk around his truck, heading straight towards my front yard. It didn't take him long to walk in the gate and up the front steps and stand before me. Markel stood a step in front of me as he leaned over onto the railing, like he was some good looking, cool dude. Alright, so what; he is good looking, and maybe he was a bit cool in my eyes. But, so what.

Markel looked in my face without saying a word to me, as I continued to pretend to be mad. Yes, I said pretend, because looking in his handsome ass face, I couldn't stay mad at him, even if I wanted to.

"Thought you were going to bed?" he asked after a few minutes of silence.

"I thought you were in the middle of doing something?"

"Where's your homegirl?"

"Where's your ratchet?"

The more he questioned me, the more I followed up with a question of my own.

"Is that why you're pretending right now?"

"Pretending to do what?"

He shook his head as a smile appeared on his face.

"Why are you acting insecure?"

"How can I be acting insecure? What reason do I have to be insecure?"

"Every time you talk to me or ask a question, it's about another female. Why you act like you're jealous of other females that be around me?"

I stood to my feet and took a step down. I stood only inches away from his face as he continued to look in my eyes.

"First, I'm not officially Markel's girl to even come close to feeling insecure about a bitch that ain't me. Second, I look too damn good to be insecure about anything. Third, I'm a proud virgin. That means, my pussy is extremely tight. That also means, I trump all those lose pussy ass bitches you fuck with. I look better, I'm stacked better, and just because I'm me. I'll make you shut all those bitches down, while I'm standing in their faces, just so they can get mad and become the insecure bitch you think I am."

"Oh, you that bold? You think you can sucker me up to do that?"

"You think I can't?"

He stood there looking in my face for a few minutes, before his eyes started to stray. His eyes ran down from my face to my perky breast, and down my thick frame, then back to my face.

"Maybe, you might be worth all that."

"Maybe? Tell me I'm worth all that."

"Aight, you're worth it."

"I know I am, and that's what you're going to do. Once you tell all those bitches to their faces that you won't be fuckin' with them anymore, I'll be yours."

"You're already mine."

"Says you…"

"Yup, I say so, but I don't mind turning them hoes down for wifey."

Markel turned and pressed his back against the railing as he grabbed my waist and pulled me into his space. I bit down on my top lip to avoid kissing him, but he seductively ran his tongue across my bottom lip.

"Mm, you gotta stop doing this to me. Because I'm not giving you none of this pussy for a long while. This right here is like teasing me, so stop it."

"If you can't take it, why even say you're gonna hold out on a nigga? Especially when you're letting me know you want me to dig deep in them guts."

"I never said that…"

"You just did…"

He kissed my lips as I melted in his arms. This nigga was too much, and he knew it. It was getting too hard for me to resist this man, but I had to. I don't want to give in and end up regretting it later. As close as I stood to him, I could feel a growing bulge. I looked down to see a huge hill forming in his pants.

"I guess I'm not the only one that's excited. What you gonna do about that, since you can't have any pussy?"

"I can't have that, but there is something you could do for me."

"Something like what? I'm not giving you head; I don't know where your dick has been." I crossed my arms over my chest, while leaning back on my left leg.

"I would never ask you to go down on me; that's what ratchets do. You could stroke it for me, though."

"Alright, I can do that. C'mon."

We went in my house and locked the door. I directed him to the kitchen to get himself some paper towels. Once he came back in the living room, I stood up as he cut the light out. I pushed him down on the sofa and climbed on top of him. We started kissing as his hands gripped my ass. I started moving my hips back and forth as he began to squeeze my ass.

I unfastened his belt and jeans, then reached inside his boxers. I pulled out his massive erection and began stroking it. Markel's dick was almost too big to fit in one hand alone. I thought about having his big ass caramel stick stuffed in my pussy and quickly got scared. But, I continued to focus on bringing him to his breaking point. We continued to kiss each other's lips deeply and passionately, as I stroked his dick a little faster.

Markel slid his hand inside my shorts and then my panties; he began rubbing his finger across my clit, sending me into a frenzy. I stroked his dick faster as he moved his fingers in a circular motion, while making my pussy wet as hell. Then he slid his fingers inside of my wetness, then started moving his hand back and forth, causing my juices to splash onto my panties. I wrapped my left arm around his neck as I stroked his dick faster, while grinding my pussy on his hands, sending his fingers deeper inside of me. "Aah, mmm…" I moaned out as he did the same. We went back and forth from moaning to kissing, until we both exploded in each other's hand.

"Shit…" My head fell on his shoulder as I held his cum in my hand, and he licked my juices off his fingers.

"You taste good. Next time I'll taste it for real." I didn't say anything as I sat up and took the paper towel out his hand. I cleaned him off first, then my hand. We promised to see each other at some point tomorrow, probably after I met up with my girls. We parted ways; Markel went home, and I headed for the shower and then bed.

CHAPTER 5

Just Wanna Get Closer To You

Zya

Saturday afternoon

I was out and about with Millian and Kitanya. We were at Seaside Park chilling—sitting on the bench by the beach. Everybody and their mama was out here. And because we finally got one warm Spring day, would you believe me if I tell you these females were walking through the park with tank tops and booty shorts with flip flops on? Shit, I wouldn't believe it myself, but they were. It almost felt like Summer, but don't let this Spring weather fool you. It wasn't hot enough to be wearing the shit half these broad had on, but to each his/ her own—I guess.

I'm sure tomorrow it'll be cold or it'll end up raining. The weather is always flip flopping on some crazy shit. Anyways, enough about the weather and these crazy bitches out here in these short shorts and shit. I was looking around watching people walk by looking crazy, but enjoying themselves, when I spotted Markel walking with a group of dudes. They were walking through the park blowing smoke (smoking blunts) with a trail of females following close behind. I peeped some female playing Markel close; Millian peeped it too.

We both were staring in his direction to see how he was going to react. But then, here goes Kitanya's nosy ass.

"Oh look, Zya there go your boo."

I rolled my eyes at KiKi, "He's not my boo, thank you very much. And you don't have to tell me; I already see him."

She continued drilling me with her words, "Uh oh, look at that ratchet all up in ya' boo's face. You should go over there and say something to him, since he gives you rides from school and whatnot."

My head swung in her direction, "Ok, and? What's your point, because you sound real sour about a situation that has nothing to do with you. You're acting real shady, like you're the one that likes him or something…"

Kitanya looked at me like she wanted to beat my ass, yet she still didn't reply to what I had said to her. To me, that said a lot. I looked at Millian, while shaking my head and giving her a look, telling her to get her girl. I don't know what's gotten into KiKi these days, but I was starting to notice how our friendship was slowly falling apart.

In the near distance, I noticed Vaughn and Jeff coming our way.

"Oh look, there's Vaughn and KiKi's abuser. Go get ya' man, bitch. He too has a ratchet damn near clinging to his skin."

56

Without saying a word, Kitanya got up and rushed over in Jeff's direction.

"I'll be right back," Millian said as she walked over to Vaughn.

I turned my head back in the direction I'd seen Markel and his lil' crew, and noticed him looking in my direction. The female was still in his ear. I'm sure she was talking a bunch of nonsense, because he didn't seem to be interested at all. Especially now that he'd noticed I was sitting here. Markel and his boys had stopped across the way on the grass. They were sitting on the tables while talking to the small group of females that followed them. Markel gestured for me to come over to where he was sitting.

Since Millian and Kitanya were busy yapping with their boyfriends, I didn't mind going to Markel and making a bitch mad. I got up from the bench, then started walking in his direction. The breeze blew through my hair, blowing some strands in front of my eyes. I took my hand and pulled my hair back out of my face. I was dressed in a pair of black sweats and a white V-neck t-shirt that had words in the front that read: *I'm the baddest Bitch!* I had on a pair of white and black Adidas to match my clothes.

Some of the dudes that were with Markel turned to look at me. I heard one of the dudes say, "*Damn, she thick.*" Then I saw a smile appear on Markel's face. As I made it over and stood in front of Markel, a few of the females turned to look at me. Some looked as if they were ready to fight me. The female standing near Markel looked in my face.

The look she had on her face was priceless, then she had the nerve to speak to me.

"Excuse you, why is you just standing there looking stupid?"

"You know, you right... Why am I standing here looking stupid?" I said without even looking in her direction.

I walked into Markel's space and slid my tongue in his mouth. We started kissing right in front of this broad. He wrapped his arms around my waist and the rest was history.

His boys were like, *"Oh shit, I bet shorty feel stupid for opening her mouth."*

Another dude was like, *"Daaaammnn, Kel, I ain't know that was your shorty."*

Then I heard a female say, *"Damn, that's real fucked up."*

Our lips parted as I turned around and gave Markel my back, then leaned back on him as he gripped my waist again, this time from behind. I decided to finally acknowledge this broad by looking at her for the first time.

"Oh, let me introduce myself. My name is Jaz'Zyazia, and in case you didn't know, Markel is my man. So, you are dismissed, shorty. Your presence ain't needed anymore."

The female's mouth dropped; she looked to be in shock. But then, her facial expression quickly switched up. She looked like she was ready to bounce in my direction.

"Bitch, I don't know who you think you are, but, I've been messing with Markel for the last six months. I ain't going nowhere!"

"Messing with him? Oh, you mean you been fuckin' him these last six months? Ok, what's your point? That has nothing to do with me. My point is, you've served your purpose. He's done with you; that means your six months of just fuckin', is ova. You're a ratchet, and he's done fuckin' with ratchets, mama."

"A ratchet? Bitch, I got ya' ratchet!" She was about to swing at me, until I started laughing. She stood there looking at me like I'd lost my damn mind.

"Wait—wait, this shit is way too funny. One thing I don't do, is fight ova a nigga, especially one that belongs to me. Second, I look way too damn good to be fighting a ratchet like you, ova my man. So, Markel, please handle ya' business and dismiss this bitch."

Markel looked the bitch dead in her face and said, "Keeda, I'm good on you. You can go."

She was like, "What the fuck is you talkin' about, you good on me? Nigga, you stupid for even letting them words part your lips!"

"That's all he needs to say, you've been dismissed."

One of the females standing at the other end of the table was like, "Yo, that is too funny. Class is over, boo. You gotta go; even I knew Markel wasn't feeling your ass. See what happens when you just walk up on a nigga and try ta' holla at him not knowing his status. Sad shit is, it's a group of you bitches over here looking sour as fuck for this bitch."

I laughed because she was addressing all the ratchets that were standing over here, trying to get with whomever they were tryna holla at.

"You know what, Sandi let's go before I punch these bitches in the face."

"That'll never happen, but yes, you can definitely go about your business."

We watched the group of females walk away, leaving about four other females besides myself, standing with their boyfriends. There were now three dudes out of the group standing alone.

One of them said, "*Y'all had to fuck shit up for us, huh? Kel, your girl must have yo' ass whipped!*"

"Nah, but at least I gotta girl, though."

"You weren't saying dat shit last week, though. Not while you had, Chanteika in yo' ear."

"She sounds like a ratchet too, with a name like that. It's cool, last week doesn't matter because that chick will get her walking papers too. That's not a problem," I said as I looked dude in his face.

"Hell, I would dismiss the other females too. You a fine ass bitch; you may be worth all that drama."

"One thing I am not, is a bitch, so you need to watch yourself."

Markel was like, "Shawn, chill out my nigga. Watch yo' fuckin' mouth; don't disrespect my girl like that."

"Damn, even got my nigga checkin' me and shit. You must be a keeper."

"C'mon, let's walk," Markel said.

We walked away from his boys without sharing another word. Markel held my hand as we walked along the sidewalk, leaving the beach and everyone in the area behind.

"Where'd your friends go?"

I had forgotten all about them as I looked around to see if I could see either one of them, but saw no one.

"I don't know; their boyfriends showed up, then they disappeared on me."

"Later for them; let's be out."

"Where are we going?" I asked. "How you just gonna leave ya' people behind?"

"Man, later for them niggas. They're with their shorties, why I can't be with mine?"

"I was just asking. You sure you ready for a relationship with me? I'm as spoiled as can be. If I can't have what I want, neither can you."

"I can handle you; I'm not worried."

We walked clear across the park to the parking lot to reach his truck. After getting in the truck, we left the park. He drove around for a while, I guess to kill time. I wasn't sure what he was doing, because he didn't say anything. As he drove, the only sound in the truck that could be heard was the music he was playing. The bass of the music was bumping so hard, that the windows vibrated as they sat halfway rolled down.

I decided to call my mother, because I hadn't received a call or text from her since yesterday. I figured she'd be tryna check up on me to see what I was up to by now. I turned down the volume of the music as I pulled out my phone. Markel looked at me like I'd just shut down his whole life.

"My bad, I'll turn it back up in a minute. Let me call my mom real quick."

"Oh, go ahead, you good. I thought you were tryna be funny." I pressed the pound button, then the number one, and then pressed the talk button to speed dial my mother's phone.

I listened to her phone ring four times, before her voicemail picked up. I tried a second time and still, she didn't answer. So, I called her best friend, Ms. Tina, which is also my mother's co-worker and my Godmother. Her phone rang twice, then I heard, "Hello."

"Hi, Ms. Tina, this is Zya. Do you know if my mother has a patient right now? She's not answering her phone."

"No, she doesn't; she's not even in right now."

"I thought she had to work all the way through, until tomorrow night?"

"That's true, but she got someone to work in her place for a few hours. She said she wanted to go home to shower and cook dinner for you."

"Oh, ok. Maybe she fell asleep, or she's still in the shower. Alright then, Ms. Tina. Thank you."

"No problem, Love. Take care." As soon as the call ended, I told Markel to go by my house before turning his music back up.

We finally reached our block, just in time to see an ambulance pulling off from the curb in front of my house. I was looking around to assess the block, to see if anything crazy had gone down, but nothing and no one looked out of place. "What the hell happened out here?" I said in a low tone. There was a small crowd of people dispersing from the street in front of my house.

CHAPTER 6

Slowly Falling Apart

Zya

Seconds later...

When we got out the truck, our neighbor, Ms. Freida, came rushing over to me.

"Zyazia—Zyazia, you need to go to the hospital now!" she said with excitement in her tone.

"Huh? Why, what's going on?" She had me confused; why was she rushing over to me like a crazy woman?

"I'm not sure why, but your mom—she's been attacked, and I heard she was either stabbed or shot. I'm not sure, but you need to be heading to the hospital! That was her in the ambulance that just pulled off."

As soon as she told me my mom was in the ambulance being taken to the hospital, my body started to tremble. My heart began to beat fast as everything around me seemed to be moving in slow motion.

"What hospital are they taking her to, do you know?" I had to force the words out of my mouth. Thinking of my mother being hurt by a random person for no reason, had all types of crazy thoughts running through my head.

"I don't know; ask the officers right there."

She pointed to a police car with two officers sitting inside. I rushed over and asked them what hospital my mother was being taken to. Once they told me, I asked Markel to take me to the hospital. Without hesitation, we got back in his truck and headed to Saint Vincent's Hospital. I didn't bother to ask the officer what had happened either. That part just slipped my mind, or was it that I just didn't care? All I wanted to do was make it to the hospital, nothing else.

My mother Marsha Robinson worked at St. Vincent's Hospital in the emergency room; she's a doctor. So, I already knew that whatever happened, they would take good care of one of their own. When we finally made it to the hospital, Markel parked his truck in the hospital's parking lot and held my hand, as we rushed inside together. As we walked up to the nurse's station in the ER lobby, I couldn't help but notice the handful of police officers huddled in two groups conversing. As soon as I made it over to the station, I saw Ms. Tina. She looked up at me with this sad look in her eyes.

"Jaz…"

"Ms. Tina, what happened to my mother? Is she alright?"

She looked over at the officers, then back at me. She got up from her chair and walked from behind the station.

"Come over here; let me talk to you." She pulled me over towards a set of chairs on the opposite side of the room, away from the police officers.

"Your mother is in surgery right now, when she came in..." Her words faded away as her head fell low, as tears filled her eyes.

"Are you ok, Ms. Tina?" She was scaring me with her reactions. Deep down, I was trying to prepare myself for Ms. Tina to drop a painful bomb on my heart.

"Jaz'Zyazia, she was covered in so much blood."

She started sobbing; her chest was rapidly moving up and down. It almost seemed like she was having a hard time breathing, but she wasn't. I placed my hand on her shoulder.

"After we spoke, I started calling your mom's phone. When I'd finally reached her, she said she was in the shower. I told her that you were trying to reach her, and she said she would call you after we hang up. But then the doorbell rang. At first, she thought it was you, thinking you had forgotten your keys. When she opened the door..." Again, her words trailed off.

"Ms. Tina, please finish. Tell me what happened to my mother."

Ms. Tina looked back towards the police officers and then back at me.

"She'd opened the door to see a familiar face. At first, she didn't say who it was, they just started arguing. After a few minutes, she attempted to close the door, but the female had done something to prevent that from happening."

"A female?"

"Her name is Shalaine..."

"SHALAINE?"

"Do you know that name?"

"Yes, I do. That's the bitch my father left us for, but go ahead, finish telling me what happened."

"I heard the female telling your mother that she wanted to speak to you on behalf of your father, something about California. Anyways, your mom politely explained that you and your father already had a conversation about it, and attempted to close the door again. Well, from what I heard, the female, Shalaine, wasn't having it. She did something to prevent your mother from closing the door on her, once again. Next thing I know, I hear scuffling in the background like they were fighting. After a few minutes, the phone went dead, and now they have your mother in surgery, fighting for her life."

"What happened, why is she in surgery? Like, what did this bitch do to my mother?"

"Marsha was stabbed multiple times in her chest and back. I'm not sure how serious her injuries are as of right now, but I'll inform the doctors that you are here and are seeking some type of information about your mom's status. But don't worry, your mom is a fighter. She'll pull through this."

"Thank you, Ms. Tina." Markel and I walked around the chairs and took a seat. I hadn't realized he was still holding on to my hand, until now. As we sat down, I looked down at his hand and then up at his face. "Thank you for coming with me, Markel. I really appreciate you being here with me."

"Don't mention it. I'll always be here for you when you need me to."

"Thank you." I hope he really meant what he said, because I'm sure my life was about to become a living hell.

After about ten minutes, Ms. Tina came out to where Markel and I were sitting, to let me know that a doctor would be out soon as my mother gets out of surgery, to give me an update on her condition. Three hours later, I still haven't heard anything from anyone, and I was becoming very impatient. My phone kept buzzing with text messages from Millian and Kitanya, asking where I was and why I wasn't answering them back. KiKi even mentioned that they were sorry for dipping on me at the park, but she needed some vitamin D. I didn't bother to answer back, because I wasn't in the mood for them right now. It didn't matter to me the reason for them leaving me sitting at the park alone. If they felt leaving me to go fuck their boyfriends was more important than being with me, then so be it.

I was more worried about my mother's current condition, and why my father was now calling my phone. I ignored his call too.

"Aren't you going to answer the phone?" Markel asked.

"No, I'm not; that's only my father calling. Why would I answer his call, when it was his bitch that stabbed my mother?"

"Maybe he doesn't know what happened. I think you should answer and see what he has to say. If you don't like what he's talking 'bout, then bang on him."

Markel was right, maybe my father didn't know about what his bitch did to my mother. Maybe she acted on her own and without him telling her to go to my house. Why would the bitch want to converse with me about anything dealing with my father, anyways? I pressed the talk button and said, "Hello," nothing but attitude could be heard in my tone.

"Hey Zya, you still not talking to me? I wanted to know if you'd like to go to dinner with me tonight, just you and me?"

"Why would I want to do that?"

"Because I'm your father, and I want to spend some time with you before I leave. Zya, we had this talk already."

"Yeah, we did, and I also explained to you that I have more important things to do."

"Zya—please, all I'm asking for is dinner…"

"No, I don't have time for all that right now, or ever! Why don't you just go to California, quietly? You and your bitch have done more than enough to fuck up my life, and my mother's life as well! Karl, stop calling my phone and go live your fuckin' life. You will never get me in the same room with you again, after what happened to my mother!"

"Your mother? What happened to your mother?"

"Don't pretend like you don't know!"

"Zyazia, where are you?"

"Why you wanna know? So you could bring ya' bitch up here to finish the job? FUCK OUTTA HERE!" I hung up in my father's face. Talking to him was a waste of time.

"Why didn't you tell him what happened?"

"He probably already knows what happened. I don't care if he does or doesn't; I'm not worried about my father! He could drop dead tomorrow, and I still wouldn't give a flying fuck about him! All of this is his fault; he cheated on my mother and left us, now look what happened. My mother is fighting for her life!"

I was so angry at my father. I hate him so much and no longer wanted anything to do with him. He could move to Canada, China even, and I wouldn't care. Markel started rubbing my hand, bringing me out of the crazy thoughts I was having about my father. I looked over at him as he spoke. "Calm down, you're getting yourself all worked up..."

Just as Markel got the last word out his mouth, I heard, "Family of Marsha Robinson." I quickly stood to my feet and turned to face the doctor that had spoken.

"I'm her daughter, Zyazia," I voiced as I walked towards the doctor with Markel by my side. When we made it over to the doctor, he shook my hand and introduced himself.

"I'm Dr. Stevens, your mother is doing fine. She's in stable condition as of right now. She's not in any danger, but we did have some complications during the surgery."

Dr. Stevens paused to take a deep breath, then he continued. "One of her lungs was punctured, but we've managed to fix the minor damage. We currently have her on a breathing machine to help her breathe easier, until we're positively sure her lung has fully healed. Then we'll take her off the machine. She was stabbed a few times, front and back. Some cuts are only minor scratches, and some wounds were deeper than the others. She has over 100 stitches down her back, and over 30 stitches in the front, from her chest to her stomach." He started to walk away when he was done, but then stopped. "Oh, sorry to have to tell you this, but your mother lost the baby."

"BABY? What baby—how far along was she?"

"She was about 16 weeks pregnant, no worries. She's still able to have more babies in the future, if she wants. Other than that, Marsha will be fine and will make a full recovery."

"Thank you, Dr. Stevens." We shook hands, then I watched Dr. Stevens walk away.

To say I was in shock would be an understatement. When the hell did my mother get pregnant, and by who? I never saw her with a man; she didn't bring anyone to the house. Shit, as far as I know, she was always working all the time. So, how the hell did she end up pregnant? I walked over to where Ms. Tina sat behind the nurse's station, since she was my mom's so-called best friend, she should know all the things I knew nothing about. I walked over and stood in front of Ms. Tina as she tapped her fingers on the computer keyboard. She looked up and saw the crazy look on my face, and she stood to her feet in a panic.

"Is everything alright? What's wrong? What happened?"

I wasn't about to beat around the bush, so I just came out with it. "Did you know my mother was pregnant?"

She stood there with this shocked look on her face for a couple minutes, but then she tried to switch up the look on her face.

"Um, I don't—I don't think so," she stuttered.

"Why are you stuttering then, if you really didn't know? I think you did know about my mother's pregnancy. Why wouldn't you? You're her best friend; you would even know who she was pregnant by. So, tell me."

Ms. Tina slowly sat back down in the chair as I stood there, waiting for her to speak.

"Ok, she did mention to me before that she had found out she was pregnant."

"By who?"

"Your father, but he doesn't know she was pregnant, and she wasn't about to tell him either."

"When the hell did they have time to mess around with each other?"

"She made time, trust. She still loved your father, and he too, still has feelings for her. They've been creeping around for a while now; your father is the one that initiated it. He wanted to be with your mother in some way. Since she wanted it too, she didn't refuse him the chance."

"So, he really didn't know about the baby?"

"I'm positive that he knew nothing about the baby, but it's possible that his girlfriend found out about your mother and father…"

"I'm sure she did, since she used me as an excuse to be at my house. I'll find out though. Thank you, Ms. Tina."

"If you need anything, I'm here for you. Don't hesitate to call me."

"I won't, thanks again." Markel and I went to the room they had my mother in.

When we walked into the recovery room, and I felt my heart

damn near stop at the sight of my mother. She had a tube going down her throat connecting her to a breathing machine. She had IVs in her arm and hand. One was pumping liquids in her body, so she wouldn't dehydrate. Another tube was pumping blood into her body, because she had lost a lot of blood, and another IV was sending medication into her to prevent her from feeling the pain. This was too much for me to bear; tears instantly started falling from my eyes and down my face, forming large wet circles on my shirt.

I walked over to my mother and gently touched her forehead.

"Mommy, what the hell happened? Why didn't you tell me you were pregnant? Why'd you keep something like that from me? I swear, I'm going to kill that bitch for doing this to you! If Daddy stays with that crazy bitch after this, I swear I'll kill his ass too. Oh, Mommy..." My voice trailed off.

When I looked down at my mother's face, her eyes were closed, but she had tears rolling down the sides of her face, forming puddles in her ears. That's when I realized, she could hear everything I was saying to her. "I love you Mommy. I'll be back tomorrow to check on you. Everything will be alright, I promise. Love you, Mama." I kissed my mother's bruised face, then left the room in tears. Markel held me close in an attempt to comfort me, as we left the hospital and headed home.

CHAPTER 7

All Is Fair in Hate & War

Zya

Minutes later...

Markel thought it was a bad idea for me to go home, knowing my mother's blood would still be all over the place. He didn't want me to see the scene of my mother's attempted murder. Yes, I said attempted murder, because that's exactly what it was. The bitch must've found out about my mother and father seeing each other, and tried to kill her out of jealousy and hate. I just can't believe she used me as an excuse to attempt to get in the house. When we pulled up to the house, there were a couple cops lingering around, going over the scene, collecting whatever evidence that could've been left behind by the other investigators.

When I got out the truck and walked up the few steps leading to the front door, they were just exiting the house. Markel and I made our way inside the house to see a puddle of blood right at the door. We had to step over the blood to enter the house. A trail of blood led the way up the small hallway towards the living room. There were family portraits on the floor covered in blood. My mother's blood was smeared on the wall going in the direction of the living room as well.

We followed the blood in the living room, where another large puddle sat on the hardwood floor. The glass table that sat in front of the sofa was broken. The glass was completely shattered, leaving nothing but the metal part sitting idle. I shook my head as I silently cried to myself out of anger. Markel walked up behind me and held me in his arms. I quickly turned to face him and fell into his embrace, allowing him to comfort me. I wanted him to make this whole scene disappear.

I wished like hell time could go back, to the point none of this shit had ever happened. Markel ran his fingers through my hair as he spoke softly in my ear, telling me everything was going to be alright. But in my heart and mind, I knew nothing would be the way he was telling me it would be. I was seeing red; I literally wanted to kill that bitch. After 20 minutes of uncontrollable crying, Markel helped me clean up the blood that trailed from the front door to the living room. It took us about five hours to get all the blood up off the floor and walls and clean up the glass off the floor.

Afterwards, I checked my phone and saw that I had a text from my father, telling me he was on his way to my house. He was the last person I wanted to see right now. Why would this man be coming to my house? I made it clear to him to stay the fuck away from me. When we were finally done, I excused myself to shower and get dressed. Before I went upstairs, Markel said he would be back. He said he was going home to wash up too.

So, when he walked out the door, I locked it and continued up the stairs. I headed straight for the bathroom. After running the water in the shower and allowing the water to heat up, I got undressed, climbed inside the shower, and allowed the heat from the hot water to blanket my body like a shield. I allowed the heat from the water to massage the stress of the day and the pain I felt from seeing my mother in her current condition, from my body and mind. Afterwards, I washed my body twice, and then rinsed the soap off and got out. I wrapped myself in a towel after drying off, and made my way into my room.

After slipping on a bra and boy-shorts, I got dressed in a black fitted shirt, a pair of black sweat pants, and black and grey Nike sneakers. I ran the towel over my wet hair a couple times, then I ran the brush through my damp hair. I brushed my hair to the back and put my hair back into a low ponytail. After putting Coco Butter lotion on my arms and face, I grabbed my lip gloss and black bomber jacket and made my way out the house onto the porch. When I got outside, Markel was already there. We were damn near dressed the same; he had on all-black too.

He had on a black shirt, black sweats, and black and white Jordans along with a black fitted hat. I looked him up and down, then smiled.

I guess we think alike, huh, I thought to myself as I continued to look in his direction.

I couldn't help but think to myself about all the things 'bout Markel that made me like him so much. He's good looking, kind-hearted, he's a real ass dude, and he's a protector. As the days passed us by, I saw things in him that only made me like him more. Usually, Markel's phone would be ringing off the hook, and seconds later, he would take off. But, since we got together today, his phone hasn't been ringing much.

I even noticed how he hasn't been trapping those trashy ass females around lately. Yeah, I peeped it. But, I'm sure they were still blowing up his phone, when he wasn't around me. Even I knew miracles don't happen overnight. We would probably end up going through hell before we can really be happy together on some long-term relationship type shit, if that's what we chose to do. But we're just starting out, so I'm willing to sit back and be patient and see where this relationship goes.

As for my father, I wasn't in the mood to see his face. I didn't even want to talk to him; he knew this already, so I don't know why he was choosing to bring himself to my house. One thing I'm not about to do, is allow him to step foot inside.

"My father is on his way here..." I blurted out.

"Aight, cool."

"No matter what happens or what he says, don't leave me alone with him, Markel."

"Long as you want me here, I'm here. I won't leave."

Just then, my father pulled up in front of the house. He parked in front of Markel's Benz truck. We watched my father get out his black on black Yukon truck and make his way over to where we were now sitting on the stairs. My father looked from me to Markel with a look on his face that spoke volumes. It was clear to me that he didn't seem to like Markel much, but he also didn't know shit about him. I was scared as hell though, but I wasn't about to show it to him.

I didn't know what would happen between the two of them. I just knew Markel had my back because he didn't leave yet. I looked from my father to Markel and noticed Markel's face was expressionless. That was even scarier than the look upon my father's face. For a while, it was quiet. Nobody was saying anything; everyone was just staring at each other. My father was making me upset, and I wasn't feeling that shit, so I decided to speak first to break the ice.

"You said you were coming over to talk, right... What do you want?"

My father's head swung around to me. I could tell he was angry, but I didn't give a fuck.

"Where's your mother?"

"I already told you where she was; why are you asking again? What—you don't believe me? She's in the hospital, thanks to you!"

"Thanks to me? I didn't put her there!"

"You, might as well have, since it was your baldheaded bitch that attacked my mother, while I wasn't home. She's lucky too, because the bitch wouldn't be breathing right now."

"You don't know what you're talking about, Zya. Shalaine has been home all day, how is she going to attack your mother? Why would she want to attack your mother? There's no reason for the drama, or the crazy shit coming out your mouth. So, watch it!"

"No, how about you watch your bitch from now on, and keep her the hell away from this house! There was no reason for her asking for me to discuss you, or going to California."

"She wouldn't come here asking for you, and she's not going with me either, so why would she come asking to talk to you about going to

California?"

"Why don't you go and ask her! While you're at it, ask her why she attacked my mother! And let her know, when I see her, I'm gonna beat her ass. As a matter of fact, every time I see her, I'm gonna fuck her up!"

"Jaz'Zyazia, watch your damn mouth!"

"Karl, I'm eighteen; I'm old enough to say whatever the fuck I want. You don't live here. You gave up being my father and telling me what to do, when you walked out of this house!" I pointed back towards the door, "So, don't try to be that man, telling me what to do."

"No matter what you say, I'm still your father, and I already told you: I won't tolerate your disrespect!"

"I won't tolerate yours, either! So, I guess we're even now... We have nothing else to talk about; you need to leave."

My father looked over at Markel again.

"Who the hell is this dude?"

I looked from my father to Markel, then back to my father.

"This dude is none of your concern, so leave."

"This dude looks like a grown ass man, so he is my concern as long as he's around my daughter!"

"You already gave up those rights, so leave!"

He completely ignored me as he continued to stare in Markel's face.

"How old are you?" he questioned Markel.

Markel replied, "Old enough…" With a sly looking smirk on his face, to further piss my father off.

The look Markel was giving my father was letting him know, he was ready for whatever move my father was about to make. They both were glancing at each other like they were ready to fight. I hope like hell things didn't go that far, but if it did, I was moving my ass out the way.

"You look old enough not to be around my child! You need to go."

"I'm not a child, I'm eighteen, and he's not going anywhere. You don't make decisions for me…"

"Zya, you're not eighteen yet, and this nigga is a grown ass man! What the fuck are you doing with a grown ass man in front of my house?"

"Your house? You don't live here, and you don't pay any bills here either… This ain't your house. Must I keep reminding you that you don't live here anymore? HELLO! Look, I'm done with all this drama. You need to go, or I'm calling the cops and letting them know you and your broad attacked my mother today."

"ZYA!" my father shouted.

"Zya nothing, bye Karl. Don't come back around here anymore, and stay the hell away from my mother. Thanks, peace out."

We watched my father turn and leave. He said nothing else; he just turned around and walked towards his truck. After a few minutes, he left. I thought for a minute that my father would turn around and beat my ass for talking slick to him, but he didn't. I no longer cared for my father the way I used to. I was more than ready to erase him from my life for what happened to my mother. I can never forgive him for this shit. Because of him, my mother has been suffering non-stop.

She went from being his wife to his side chick, and he was fine with that. It seemed like my mother was good with that too, since she got to be with him in some way. I don't know what is to come after tonight. I just know I better not ever see that baldheaded, rag doll looking ass bitch, Shalaine. I was ready to knock this bitch's head off her shoulders. Every time I thought about my mother lying in that hospital bed, I wanted to badly stomp that bitch out.

"You good?" I heard Markel ask me.

"Yeah, I'm good. I'm not worried about my father. He can go fuck himself."

"Let's go inside; it's getting chilly out here."

We got up off the steps and walked inside the house. I locked the door, then accompanied Markel to the living room. We took our jackets off and turned the television on. After channel surfing, we couldn't find anything to watch. We settled for music videos on MTV. We weren't really watching them, instead they were watching us as we conversed throughout the night, until we fell asleep on the sofa. We were cuddled up on the sofa, knocked out cold. I was way too comfortable lying here with Markel, as he firmly wrapped his arms around me, and I did the same.

CHAPTER 8

Friends Ain't Real

Zya

Early afternoon, next day

I was awakened by a call from Millian about an hour ago. She wanted to come over, and honestly, I wasn't in the mood to be around any of my friends after yesterday. I've been so stressed dealing with my parents and this crazy situation between them, I was feeling lost and confused. Somehow, I was going to get through everything. Anyways, I agreed to meet up with Millian at my house. Maybe I needed to be around my friends to ease some of the stress and pain I was feeling. She was supposed to be here within the hour, and here I was still lying here on the sofa being lazy.

Markel had already left before I woke up. I figured he had some things to do that didn't involve me. I wasn't the clinging type anyways; I wasn't about to have him trapped up under me all the time. But, it would've been good to know where he was. I got my lazy ass up off the sofa and went upstairs to the bathroom to brush my teeth. Afterwards,

I went in my room and ran a comb and brush through my hair.

Soon as I stepped out into the hallway from my bedroom, I heard the doorbell ring twice. I made my way downstairs to open the door. When I opened the door, Millian was standing there with Kitanya and Jeff. I put my hand on my hip as I looked at KiKi, because she already knew not to bring this nigga to my house. She wasn't allowed here with him, but here she was standing here with Jeff like shit was all good.

Millian said, "I told her not to bring him, but you know this bitch hard of hearing…"

"Well then, she shouldn't've come here at all." I turned to look Jeff in his face, "You can't be here, so you gotta go."

"What I do?" he quizzed.

"You and Kitanya already know my mother don't want you here after the disrespectful shit y'all did last time. You can't be here; you gotta go," I said with a bit more attitude.

"My bad, I've been meaning to apologize to your mom. It was out of my hands; I can't always control this girl's actions."

"Oh, so you're saying it was KiKi that wanted to keep going, knowing my mom was right there." He silently shook his head. I looked at Kitanya, "Y'all both have to go. You're not allowed here anymore. We can meet somewhere else, but right now—you gotta go."

She smiled, "That's fine, see ya."

She turned and walked away with Jeff following right behind her. She made her way out the gate and up the block.

All I could do was shake my head as I looked at Millian and said,

"This bitch got some shit wit' her... I can't—I just can't do it no more; she can't be around me. She's too fuckin' funny acting with me, and now to know she did that shit on purpose in front of my mother. I should've just punched that bitch in the face. What's her problem?"

Millian continued to stay silent; she was just as confused as I was. We walked inside the house, and I closed the door and told Millian to come with me in the kitchen. When we made it to the kitchen, I walked over to the refrigerator.

"You hungry?"

"Nah, I'm good... Where's your mom, she still working?" Millian asked.

I felt my heart drop to the bottom of my stomach. I hadn't talked about my mother since the argument with my father last night. I tried so hard not to think about what happened to her. But, nobody will let this shit die down so that I can forget about it. I don't want to keep thinking about this situation. I just want my mom to get better and come home. That is all.

I stood in front of the refrigerator with my back turned towards Millian. I didn't say anything, and I didn't move. I was standing there with my head hanging low, trying to fight back the tears that were building in my eyes.

"Are you alright?" Millian asked.

I turned and looked in her face, not knowing what to say. I'm sure she could tell that my emotions were all over the place. I was angry with my father, and felt an unimaginable amount of pain in my heart for my mother's current situation. I didn't know whether I should cry or break something.

"How about, you take a deep breath and tell me what happened to your mom."

"After y'all bitches left me hanging, Markel offered to bring me home. Only we didn't come straight here. He decided to drive around for a bit, but then when we got here an ambulance was just pulling off. My neighbor, Ms. Freida, told me it was my mother. Long story short, my mother was attacked in our house, and now she's laid up in the hospital, fighting to stay alive."

"Are you serious—who attacked her?"

"Her best friend said it was my father's bum-ass girlfriend. And get this, after speaking to the doctor, hearing about my mother's condition and state she was in when she came in, to the point of them saving her life, he tells me that the baby didn't make it…"

"Baby? What baby, Ms. Robinson was pregnant?"

"That's the same shit I said. I didn't even know my mother was pregnant. She was like 16 weeks or some shit. I had to confirm this information with my mother's best friend, because I didn't believe it. But, when she confirmed it and told me the baby belonged to my father of all people… I was pissed the fuck off; I wanted to kill him. Like, why the fuck would you leave my mother in the first place and claiming to be filing for divorce, only to keep fuckin' her and stringing her along? Because of him, my mother almost lost her life!"

"Did you speak to him about all of this, does he know about the loss of the baby?"

"My mother never even got to tell him about the baby to begin with. What I'm tryna figure out is, what this bitch's motives were for coming here and attacking my mother."

"She needs her ass beat for that shit! Did she know about the baby?"

"I doubt it."

"Then she must've found out about your parents still being involved with each other."

"Anything is possible, but how that look—the side bitch being mad at the main bitch for fuckin' around with the nigga she's still married to from the start? That shit is fun-ty. I just know, when I catch that ho, I'm gonna beat the shit outta her."

"Well, I'm right there with you. Whenever you're ready, shit... Ms. Robinson don't deserve the mess she received, especially not from some damn side bitch!"

"I just know this shit got me stressed the fuck out, and this ain't even the last of it..."

"Wait, there's more?"

"I wish there wasn't more, but—" I was interrupted by the sound of my phone buzzing in my pocket, due to receiving a text message. When I looked at the message, I saw that the message was from Kitanya

KiKi: I thought that shit you pulled was corny. I'll see you alone soon enough.

I looked down at my phone like I could smell this bitch's stank breath through the screen. I was surprised by the bullshit I was reading; the way she was coming at me was crazy.

"Wow, Millian, I think your girl is wildin' out right now."

"Who, KiKi? What she talkin' 'bout?"

"She just said I was wrong for what I did, and that she'll see me when I'm alone. She crazy for that, like she could beat my ass..."

"We're all friends; we're too close like sisters for her to be coming at you like she ready for a one-up (fight). I'll talk to her later."

"Nope, you don't have to talk to nobody. She's gonna do what she wants anyways. It's obvious that she's feeling some type of way. Her feelings have nothing to do with me, but if she feels that I'm the one she wants to take her issues out on... That's cool too, do you boo."

My phone buzzed again. When I looked at the screen, I saw that it was Markel this time. He was asking me what I was doing. I let him know I was about to go visit my mother. He told me to come outside. Guess I wasn't making nothing to eat right now. A few minutes after receiving Markel's text, Millian and I went outside to see Markel waiting by his Benz truck.

I locked the door, then we walked over to where Markel was. Markel kissed my lips, then opened the passenger door for me. He opened the back door for Millian too.

"Well damn, ain't you a gentleman. Thank you, Markel." Once Millian got in and Markel closed the door, Millian was like, "You got'chu a good nigga; maybe that's why KiKi be hating on him so hard."

Millian doesn't know Markel been saying that same shit. I don't care what Kitanya's issue is with Markel or me; she just needs to get over it and move on with her life. Markel got in the truck, and we were on our way to see my mother. On the drive to the hospital, we laughed and joked around. It was all fun and games, but without KiKi's crazy behind, it wasn't the same. Damn, she really knew how to fuck shit up.

It was Sunday; the weekend was finally coming to an end. We still had the week of no school to look forward to, then it was back to focusing on making straight A's and start preparing for graduation in June. I wasn't looking forward to going back to school no time soon, though. That would mean I would have to see Kitanya's ass all damn day. For her, it wasn't good with all the shit she was starting up.

I was staring out the window at the scenery passing me by. Millian was in the backseat talking a mile a minute. I felt Markel's hand touch my thigh. I guess he was tryna get my attention, but I was too busy looking out the window with a thousand things on my mind. I didn't even hear him calling out my name.

"Zya—Zyazia, what's good, Ma?" He gently squeezed my leg, again to get my attention. I turned to look at him.

"Huh?"

"What's on your mind? I called you twice and still you couldn't hear me."

"Oh, my bad… I'm just thinking about everything that's been going on these last few days."

"Like what?"

"This shit with my mother and father, this bitch Kitanya and her dry ass threat, my relationship with my father—shit like that."

Millian said, "Zya, don't let this shit with KiKi get to you. I told you that I'll talk to her; there's no reason for y'all to get crazy over nothing."

"We don't even know what '*nothing*' is, fuckin' with that damn girl. She just wants to start shit, because her shit with Jeff ain't going as she planned. That has nothing to do with me. Fuck her! I have more important shit to worry about, and she ain't it."

I took a deep breath and turned back around to continue looking out the window. This shit with Kitanya didn't bother me one bit. I knew this shit would happen one day; I knew it would be her to make me not like her ass or trust her ever again. Like I said, fuck that bitch. If she wants problems with me, she can get it. As of right now, I'm unbothered by that bitch.

She's the last person I care to think about. Markel pulled into the hospital's parking lot and quickly found the nearest parking space, which wasn't far from the hospital's entrance. We got out the truck and made our way inside. After walking inside the hospital, it didn't take us long to ride the elevator up to the seventh floor, where my mother was staying. When we stepped off the elevator, Markel and I were walking hand in hand with Millian walking beside us. We walked up to the end of the corridor to my mother's private room.

I prayed that her condition had gotten a little better today, because I couldn't take seeing her like that. She was covered in bruises, and she had all those IVs and tubes down her throat. We walked in the room to see my father in there standing by the foot of my mother's hospital bed, and his girlfriend sitting in a chair in the corner. I quickly released Markel's hand and rushed in the room, passed my father, and straight over to his girlfriend. I grabbed that bitch by the four inches of hair she had left on her head and yanked her head forward.

"BITCH, YOU GOT SOME DAMN NERVE BEING UP IN HERE!" I swung a closed fist to the right side of her face, as my left hand still held her hair.

I heard Markel and Millian both say, "*Oh, shit!*" at the same time.

Then as my father turned in my direction, he said, "Zya, let her go!" He grabbed my hands as Millian and Markel rushed over to help my father get me off this bitch.

"Let me go! Lil' girl, what the fuck are you doin'? You so, damn—OUCH!"

I punched that bitch in her mouth. "SHUT THE FUCK UP, HO!"

I hit her a good three times, before my father successfully pulled me off her. Markel pulled me away from my father, towards the door.

"What are you doing? You're hitting a grown woman! Are you crazy?" my father yelled at me.

"Nigga, are you fuckin' crazy bringing her here after she did that shit to my mother? Nah, you must be fuckin' dumb! GET HER THE FUCK OUTTA HERE! Your ass shouldn't even be here either; both of y'all can get the fuck out!"

Two nurses came rushing in the room with a doctor I've never seen before.

"WHAT'S GOING ON IN HERE?" the doctor shouted.

"They're not supposed to be in here; that's the lady that attacked my mother! Get security and police officers up in here, before I beat her ass again!"

The nurses and doctor looked over in my father and Shalaine's direction. "Excuse me, but you have to go, sorry… If it's true that this woman attacked, Mr. Robinson, she can't be in here. Please wait in the hallway for security to come."

My father and Shalaine attempted to walk by me, but as soon as she got near me, I swung at her again, hitting her in the face.

"Stupid bitch—fuck outta here!" I said as she gripped her face, while my father attempted to shield her from me.

Didn't he already realize it was too late? I'd already popped that bitch in her face; I just wished she would've fought back. I wanted her to try to fight me back, so that I could demolish her ass. My father is on some dumb shit for bringing that bitch up here and thinking it was ok. That man must've slipped and cracked his skull, to think it was perfectly fine to bring that bitch in here to see my mother. I bet my mother would probably do the same thing, if she were able to move around.

She would beat the bloody snot out that bitch, and make it to where she couldn't breathe. She'd probably beat the dumb ass bitch to death. If I'd had the chance, I would do the same thing. When I calmed down, I walked over to the side of my mother's bed. I'd noticed they'd taken the breathing tube out her mouth, and some of the bruises on her face were getting lighter. That meant they were starting to heal.

When I looked at my mother's face, she looked like she was happy—stress free. She didn't look like she was sad or in pain; she looked happy. And you know what, I was happy too—fuck it. I was happy that I got to whoop Shalaine's ass real quick. I was happy that I didn't have to hear Kitanya's big ass mouth complaining about every damn thing. I was happy my father's dumb ass wasn't standing in my face, pretending to give a fuck about my mother being laid up in this hospital.

He was a done deal—a wrap; he could never turn back and think of us as part of his family again. The only family he has is the bitch he left with. I gently grabbed ahold of my mother's hand and began massaging it in a circular motion.

"Don't worry, Ma, I'm not finished with that baldheaded weasel. I'm gonna beat her down every single time I run into her, for what she did to you. Daddy can play the fool for her, but I won't. It's not gonna happen," is all I said.

Millian and I took turns talking to my mother for a few hours, then Markel went to drop her off. When I was alone with my mother, I started talking to her about Markel. I wondered if she'd remember everything I was saying to her when she wakes up. Why ain't she waking up yet anyways?

CHAPTER 9

My Family or My Bitch

Karl

Sunday night

"*I* told you not to follow me up there, didn't I?" I yelled at Shalaine.

"Oh, well! I told your ass not to go up there to begin with. Why would you care about your ex-wife being in the hospital?"

"My wife—she's still my fuckin' wife; get that through your nappy head! Don't worry about what I do, that's my family! I'm gon' always check up on my family; speaking of which... Why'd you go to her house?"

"What're you talkin' 'bout? I never went over there; I have no reason to go over there."

"You're lying!" I shouted out of anger.

"No, I'm not! Why would you feel I'm lying to you?" She stood up from the chair she was sitting in. "See, your problem is that you're always defending them, and for what? You're not even living with them anymore! Remember, you left your family behind for me!" Why she felt that way, I have no clue. That's not the truth at all.

"Dat don't mean shit to me; I'll leave yo' ass and go back to my family! You ain't stopping me from doing nothing I don't want to do. And get your facts straight: you were never a part of the reason I was separated from my family!"

"You probably were fuckin' your daughter's mother all this time anyways; I don't put it past you. You're very capable, with your sneaky ass..."

"Bitch, I'm a grown ass man; the fuck I need to sneak around for?"

"Bitch? Ok, so then tell me the truth... Were you still fuckin' your daughter's mother behind my back?"

"Yup, every day since we separated. You satisfied? We've been messing around from the first night we broke up, until a couple days back. Now, I find out you'd gone over there and attacked my wife. I should kill yo' ass right now!"

"You son-of-a-bitch!" Shalaine shouted out, with anger filling each word that came out her mouth.

"What? You thought you were something special? You're not! You're just a side bitch that can always be replaced or thrown away! I didn't leave my wife and daughter because of yo' ass... I left, because my wife and I were having too many problems, and I needed time away. I had no real plans on divorcing my wife and leaving my family behind. But then, you came along and started clinging to a nigga, and now look what happened… You went and done some dumb shit!"

"I did what I did, for us! She was tryna break us apart; I couldn't have that!" Her voice was full of rage, but then she quickly switched up and calmed her tone. "She needed to stay in her lane and know her place."

"Know her place? Shit, do you know yours? You not wifey, muthafucka!"

"What?"

"You got a ring on your finger? NO, right? Stay in your muthafuckin' place! Who the hell are you to even spit those words out your mouth? You were a desperate secretary looking for a come up, so you climbed your lil' skinny ass in my pockets and made a home. Whelp, it's all over for you."

"What's all over? I know you're not tryna—" I cut her off.

"You're done—your time is up—it's the end of the line—your time has expired—you're fired, bitch! I don't need you in my house or place of business anymore! If I see you again, I'll whoop your ass myself for attacking my wife. You won't have to worry about my daughter jumping on you again; you got me to worry about now! Get yo' lil' bit of shit, and get the fuck out my house!"

"Wait a minute, Karl you're doing too much… You're just mad; when you calm down, you won't be saying all this mess. I'll leave for a few hours and come back. When you're calm, I'll come back, and then we can figure this out." She was speaking fast, and her voice was a bit shaky as she spoke.

"Get yo' shit and bounce ain't shit to figure out!"

She rushed towards me with her arms reaching out for me. "Karl—baby, please wait!"

Soon as she got close enough to me, I mushed her back by her face.

"Nah, take dat shit to someone else's doorstep. I ain't trying to hear all that noise; just get the fuck out! Matter fact, don't touch nothing; I'll UPS your stuff to you! Go back to your room in your mother's basement, where you belong. I'm done dealing with you. I won't say no more—GET OUT!"

I folded my arms across my chest, waiting for her to say another word, so I could knock her across her face and carry her out to the curb like a pile of trash. Shalaine knew not to fuck with me, but for some reason, she tried her hand with my wife. Since I don't have the real story, I had no clue on what the fuck really happened. All I know is, my daughter is done wit' me, and my wife is laid up in the hospital, unconscious. The same hospital I got kicked out of about an hour ago. I tried to let Zya know this situation was temporary.

I wanted my wife and daughter back in my life badly, but it wasn't going to happen. Not if Jaz'Zyazia had something to say about it. I'd fucked up with my wife a while ago. True, I got caught cheating by my wife at my office, but it wasn't with Shalaine. In fact, the female I'd cheated with, didn't even work at my office. She didn't even work in the building.

Yeah, she's an attorney too, but not from my firm. Her name is Kachecali; she's about 5'7 or 5'8. She has a nice body, but not better than my wife. Her D-cup breast were nice and firm; she's shaped like a Coca-Cola bottle, with wide hips and a fat ass. Her eyes are brown, if I'm not mistaken, and her hair was long, past her shoulders, and the color was auburn the last time I'd seen her. She's a tanned, Puerto Rican freaky Mami that I met in court.

In fact, she was the prosecutor fighting against one of my clients in a criminal case. I ended up winning the case, and she ended up buying me dinner that night. That same night, we got a room and fucked for a few hours, then I went home. We fucked a few times after that; each time we were done, I would get up and go home to my wife and daughter. The first time, I felt guilty about what had happened. But by the third time, I didn't care.

We kept it going for about two weeks to a month, before I got caught fucking Kachecali on my desk in my office. Marsha and Kachecali got into a crazy fist fight. I didn't know what to do or say at the time; all I could do was watch, because Kache was fighting my wife, while being ass naked. What man wouldn't enjoy seeing that shit? After my wife sent her home with a black eye, busted lips, and bloody nose, I hadn't heard from her again. A week and a half later, I ended up fucking around with Shalaine, my personal secretary.

Once she got a taste of my good dick, she didn't want to let go of it. Eventually, my wife caught wind of Shalaine; Marsha was finally fed up with my shit. I got booted out of the home I'd paid for, and was forced to purchase a two-bedroom house of my own. Thus, to say, this is the reason Shalaine is still around fucking up my life now. I had to get rid of her, because she was nothing but poison. Her own family didn't want her around them either, because of her crazy ways. They could've at least warned a nigga about how violent she gets when she doesn't get her way.

I've never introduced Shalaine to my family, because she's just not the type of chick you bring around your peoples like that. She's also not someone I planned to spend my life and all my time with either. My daughter Zyazia is always calling her ugly and baldhead. Yeah, it's true, she has a short haircut, which doesn't fit the shape of her round face. She has pretty brown eyes and full lips. Her head doesn't match her body—hell, her body doesn't match her body. She's a little top heavy, but her bottom is a lil' petite.

Her waist is medium, and she has a small booty. Her belly ain't all that big, but she does have a little pudge. But again, she has the prettiest brown eyes. Other than that, she looks like a pear that someone has bitten into in random spots—if you know what I mean—making her body look uneven. She wasn't all that ugly—I guess. Shit, she was fuckable, and I wasn't complaining, because I was the dumb nigga that was fucking her for the last six months or so, since my wife tossed me out the house. I was going to move to Cali for a fresh start, but just recently cancelled my plans, when me and my daughter's relationship started to crumble.

I thought I would let Zya know I'd cancelled my plans for California over dinner or something, but she's not fucking with me right now. She doesn't want to be around a father like me, so she's writing me off as just another lame ass nigga that has done wrong by her mother. I don't know how I'm going to correct my mistakes, but I got to figure out something fast before I lose my family, completely. I know Zya said to basically make myself disappear, but I can't do that. Ain't no way in hell I was about to leave my family behind. I don't care 'bout how many times I said I was bouncing; I'm not going nowhere. I also wanted to know who this lil' nigga is that Zya is around.

He looks to be way older than her and dresses like one of them street niggas, blinged out in gold chains and diamonds. I wasn't feeling him being around her—nah, not my Zya. All these young niggas looked for in a female was a wet pussy and banging body. Not with my daughter; he gotta go—like, yesterday. Zya is going to hate me even more, but I'll take that. After all, I am her father, not one of her friends.

I was finally alone in the house without Shalaine's aggravating voice barking in my ear. Outside, the sun was starting to set, and without the lights on, the house was growing dark. I was sitting in my favorite black leather recliner with my head laid back. My eyes were closed as I thought of the day. Zya was saying Shalaine had gone over and attacked my wife. I had to remember if Shalaine was really in the house that day. I'd had a day off from work and was cleaning my house. I'd cooked for myself—something I always did, since Shalaine can't cook at all.

Even though I was in the house most of the morning, I realized that I did leave out the house to run by my office to get some paperwork for a case I was working on. I'd spent an hour at my office, before coming back home. When I got home that day, Shalaine wasn't here. When she got back that evening, she was dressed differently from when I'd left early that afternoon. It was possible that Shalaine could have done what Zya was accusing her of. We won't know the true story of what happened, until my wife Marsha wakes up.

~VENOMOUS~

Zya

Introductions

Once again, Markel and I had gone to see my mother at the hospital. When we made it to her floor, we ran into her doctor as soon as we stepped off the elevator. He told me that my mother was conscious and talking, it's like she was never hurt. That was good news for me, but now, I was also nervous because that meant Markel and my mother would be meeting for the first time. My mother and father were different in every way possible, but she didn't play when it came to me. Before, I was single and wasn't worried about having a boyfriend.

Now look at me: I had Markel. My father doesn't like the thought of Markel being around me, and doesn't even know that Markel and I are now a couple. How will my mother react when she finds out? Only one way to find out. I thanked my mother's doctor for that bit of good news he'd given me, and continued my short journey to my mother's room with Markel by my side. When we made it to the room, I stopped just outside the door. I took a deep breath as Markel looked at me.

"You alright?"

"I'm nervous…"

"Nervous about what?"

"You and my mother meeting for the very first time. My father already dislikes you; I don't want my mother to feel the same way."

"Let's go inside and find out…"

"You're not nervous?"

"Nah, I'm a likeable type of dude. I think your mom will like me; she's not your father." I shook my head in silence as we walked past the threshold into the room.

My mother was accompanied by her best friend, Ms. Tina. They were talking and laughing up a storm. My mother was trying not to laugh too hard.

"Oh girl, stop, you're killing me. I can't laugh anymore: this shit hurts like hell,"

I heard her say to Ms. Tina. Markel and I walked further into the room, where we could be seen.

"Hey Mommy, glad to see your finally up. You were scaring me for a minute."

My mother's eyes grew wide with excitement when she saw me.

"Hey, my Love. I heard you were up here every day since I've been here."

"Every day, all day. You know I wasn't about to have you up here all alone."

"Sorry for scaring you like…" Her words trailed off as her eyes focused on Markel. "And who is this fine, young gentleman?"

"Hi Mrs. Robinson, I'm Markel Spencer." He reached out for my mother's hand, and she reached back, placing her hand in his.

She gripped his hand tightly; without letting go, she asked him, "Are you dating my daughter?"

I looked over at Markel as he looked at me, then back at my mother. "Mom, I—." She cut in and cut me off.

"Nope, not talking to you. I'm speaking to Markel; mind ya' business."

"Well, alrighty then…" I said as I walked over to the empty chair over in the corner and sat down.

"Yes, ma'am. I'm dating your daughter; I hope that's not a problem for you."

"How old are you, Markel?"

"Twenty-three…" Markel replied.

She was staring deeply into his eyes as she continued to speak, "Are you a high school dropout?"

"No ma'am, graduated with honors."

"Got a job?"

"I used to have an honest job, but wasn't getting honest pay, nor was I being treated fairly. I'll be honest with you, Mrs. Robinson… If you consider being a street pharmacist a job, then yes, I do. Regardless of what I do, I'm a good dude, I'm very respectful, and I'm honest. I care about your daughter a lot. She'll never be exposed to what I do. So, you don't have to worry about any of dat."

"Where are your parents, Markel?"

"My mother died a few years back, and my father ain't never been a part of my life. The only family I deal with is my older sister; her name is Kim."

"Oh, do you have other family around besides your sister?"

"I do, but I don't be around them like that. Me and my family don't get along that well. At least my father's side. My mother's side of the family is from Brooklyn; we kind of fell out of touch after my grandparents passed away a year ago. So, it's just me and my sister out here."

"You don't have any kids already, do you?"

"Nope, I don't have any kids. Hope to have one or two, when I settle down and get married."

"You know all the right things to say, huh?"

"Just speaking truthfully…"

"Well, I heard you've been here every day with my daughter. She must like you a lot to bring you up here like this, so I'll give you a chance, and thank you for being there for her."

"No need to thank me, Mrs. Robinson. Even if I weren't with Zya, I would still look out for her. We're neighbors."

"Ooh, you're the boy with the nice truck from next door, that's always parking in my parking spot in front of my house?"

"My bad, but yeah that's me." He smiled.

My mother and Mrs. Tina busted out in laughter.

"Markel, don't pay my mother no mind. Just know, she likes you."

"Yes Markel, I do like you, but if you hurt my daughter… I'm gonna hurt you; keep that in mind. I won't tell my daughter who she can and cannot date. She's old enough to make her own decisions; just don't break her heart."

"You need to tell Mr. Robinson that. The man seems to think he has a right to speak on how I move. I don't like that man, or his ugly, baldheaded monkey!" I blurted out, out of anger and frustration.

"Oh, you've met my husband, Markel?"

Before Markel could answer, I said, "Yeah, right..."

Then Markel said, "Unofficially... I met him in the middle of a situation between him and Zya. He already cast judgement against me at that time. He doesn't like me as the person being with his daughter. Says I'm too old and look like a street nigga."

"He said that?"

"Sure did!" I added.

"Your husband is so disrespectful," Ms. Tina chimed in. My mother said nothing; she just sat there shaking her head.

I wanted to ask my mother about the baby and messing around with my father, but chose not to touch that topic, until she was back home. As bad as I wanted to know what the hell was going on between her and my father, I left it alone. I didn't want to get into an arguing match with my mother in front of Ms. Tina and Markel. Speaking of Markel, do you believe him and my mother conversed the entire time, until visits were over? She must really like him. Sometimes, I wish my father was more like my mother. But he's not; he's the type to judge a person by their looks, without knowing what type of person they really are. He ain't shit!

CHAPTER 10

Finally, Home

Marsha

Four days later

I hoped Jaz'Zyazia would have a relaxing spring vacation, but because of me and all that had happened, she was busy worrying about me the entire time and unable to enjoy herself. I'm not sure how long she and Markel have been dating, or how long they'd even liked each other. But, he seems like a nice young man. He really seems to care about my young Zya. I don't care about what he does in the streets. As a parent, I should be more concerned about who my daughter is dating.

But, Zya is just like me. I can't stand for people to be all up in my business, especially my parents. I'm more concerned about how she's being treated. Long as he keeps her safe and out of harm's way, I'm good. Long as he doesn't get my Zya mixed up in that street shit, I'm good. As far as my husband Karl goes, he'll just have to get over himself and mind his damn business.

Karl always seems to have a lot to say about everything, since he's been living the single life, while still being married. What he needs to think about is how I'm going to handle his bitch, when my body is completely done healing, and I could move a bit easier. As of now, my movement is limited. I wasn't trying to bust any of these stitches I still had in my upper back and chest areas. Before leaving the hospital not long ago, the doctor had removed the stitches in my lower abdomen and my lower back. I had a scar down my left cheek from when I fell into the glass table in my living room.

Somehow, I got cut—not sure how, because at the time, I wasn't focused on all the details of this bitch attacking me. I was busy trying to stay alive, while this damn female was replaying a scene out of *Child's Play*. Ugh, I don't even want to think about that shit anymore; I just want to go in the house and get in my bed. Markel was nice enough to drive me home from the hospital. We were just pulling up in front of the house. Once he parked the car, both Markel and Zya helped me out the car and into the house.

They helped me up the stairs to my bedroom. When we made it to my bedroom, Markel excused himself, allowing Zya to help me to bed. Zyazia helped me out of my hospital clothes and into a large pajama shirt, then she helped me get in the bed.

"Do you need anything, Mommy?"

"Can you make me some lemon tea and a salad? I'm not really that hungry, but my stomach is talking."

"Alright, I'll be back in a few with your salad and tea. Call me or text my phone if you need anything else."

I watched Zya walk out my room, closing my door behind her as she left out. When she left, I picked up my phone off my bed and texted my husband.

Me: *I don't appreciate all the shit that bitch did to me. And I don't appreciate you bringing her to the hospital, either. Fuck you and her!*

I placed my phone back on the bed, then tried to stretch towards the nightstand to retrieve the remote control. It was a painful struggle, but I finally got it. I turned on the television and found that Denzel Washington's movie John Q was on TV. I settled for this movie, because it was one of my favorite Denzel Washington movies. My phone vibrated, alerting me of the new text message I'd just received. I picked up my phone and looked at the message, noticing it was from my husband.

Him: *I apologize to you, because I knew nothing about what happened. I'm no longer seeing her and would like to see you, if you don't mind. I'd like to talk to you face-to-face.*

I responded back to his message.

Me: *I don't know if I'm ready for a face-to-face with you just yet. Thank her for me for making me lose your baby; at least I don't have to abort it. Goodnight, Karl!*

I added the part about an abortion, but I was never thinking about getting an abortion after I found out about the baby. I'm not the type of person that would kill a fetus; that's like committing murder. I would never harm anyone, let alone a helpless, growing baby. Zya walked in the room with a cup of warm lemon tea and a bowl of salad. She walked around the bed and handed me the bowl of salad; it had sliced cucumbers, thin slices of carrots, and chopped up purple cabbage, along with regular pieces of lettuce.

Zya placed the tea on the table. "If you need anything, text me. I'll be downstairs with Markel; we'll be sitting outside on the steps."

"Alright, I'll do that. Don't get yourself in any trouble."

"Huh? I won't… I'll be right outside. Keep your phone close to you, just in case."

I watched Zya walk out the room, once again. After eating my salad, I got tired and began dosing off as I tried to continue watching my movie on TV. I was in the sitting position in bed, and the sheets were covering my body from the waist down. I leaned my head back and fell fast asleep. As I slept uncomfortably on my bed in the sitting position, I had a dream of that day all this crazy shit went down.

I walked downstairs as the doorbell sounded off, echoing through the house. I could see myself, as if I were having an outer body experience. I watched myself walk to the door. When I opened the door, I was face-to-face with my husband's so-called girlfriend, Shalaine. She was dressed in a black shirt, black sweat pants, and white sneakers.

She had the tiniest ponytail atop her head. She was saying something to me, but I couldn't hear what she was saying. I tried to close the door, but she prevented me from doing so. She started speaking again, while waving her hands in my face. I was dressed in panties and a bra, covered by a house robe, so I wasn't trying to get into a confrontation at my front door. I was telling her to back up out my house.

Her mouth was still moving, and I still couldn't hear what she was saying. Next thing I knew, she was charging towards me with a big ass knife in hand. I attempted to fight her off, while trying to catch her hand that held the knife, in mid-air. I completely failed at my attempt. I felt the knife continuously digging into my skin. Each time the knife penetrated my body, I felt warm trickles of blood sliding down my skin. The pain was so intense, that I pushed her backwards and tried to run towards my living room to the house phone to call 9-1-1.

I didn't make it; she caught me a few seconds later in the hallway, a few steps away from the door. She stabbed me in my back a few times, and I screamed out and ran. Once I finally made it to my living room, after being stabbed more than a few times in my back, Shalaine grabbed me by my hair and yanked my head back. I instantly twisted my body around and grabbed both her arms. We fought for no more than five minutes, before she began stabbing me again. I didn't know where the knife was hitting me at; I just felt the pain. When she was done, she pushed me off her; I ended up losing my balance and fell backwards into the glass table that sat in front of the sofa in the living room.

Upon impact, I hit my head on something hard and then blacked out. I never did get to call 9-1-1.

When I saw myself hit the table, my eyes popped open. I could feel sweat running down the side of my face and anger fill my body. My heart was racing as pain jolted through my body like electricity. I was about to call for Zya, but chose not to. Instead, I took a few deep breaths and tried to forget my dream, as well as the entire situation that happened.

~VENOMOUS~

It's About Time

Zya

After giving my mother her salad and tea, Markel and I went outside and sat on the porch for a lil' while. The sun was hiding behind the clouds as it began to set. I cuddled up close to Markel, leaning my head on his shoulder as he wrapped his arm around me. Thanks to the sun playing peek-a-boo, a cold breeze blew across my face. Why did we choose to come out here; better yet, why is the sun hiding? When I checked the weather earlier, it said that it would be close to 70 degrees and feeling a little like Summer.

Told you, this weather is funny, but it's cool because I got Markel to keep me warm. We cuddled up and began to converse, while trying to chillax and enjoy each other's company—not noticing the three girls and two dudes walking up to my gate. We finally saw them as they reached my yard and stopped in front of the gate. Out of the five-people standing in front of us outside the gate, I notice Kitanya standing in the middle of the two girls—front and center. She had this funny look on her face that told me she was here looking for trouble.

I didn't say nothing at first; I sat there still cuddled up with Markel. He looked down at me, but I didn't look up at him. I kept my eyes trained on Kitanya, to see what she was about to do. They all stood there not saying nothing, so I turned my eyes away from them and gave Markel my full attention.

In a low tone, he said, "Ain't dat ya' girl?"

"Nah, she's not my girl anymore; she's too damn disrespectful," I answered.

"Why she here with all those people then? She here to start some shit wit' you, or something?"

"Guess so… She knows she don't pump fear over here. I ain't even on that shit right now; I don't even know why she here."

Out of nowhere, Kitanya speaks up.

"You know exactly why I'm here. Didn't I say I was gon' see you?"

"Ok, you see me, and now you can go. Don't bring your drama over here; don't nobody got time for that."

"That's your problem; you think you could tell everybody what to do."

"Fuck is you talking about, Kitanya? I've never even attempted to boss you, so why are you standing there making shit up? You need an excuse to be a bully now? I'm not around for your shit, bounce!"

She walked through the gate and one of the females followed her. I quickly stood to my feet, because I wasn't about to allow Kitanya and this girl to jump me. I took off my jacket and tossed it on the porch towards the door.

"You walking up in here with this bitch, like y'all 'bouta try ta' run up on a bitch. KiKi, don't get knocked on ya' ass. I'm not tryna go there with you, cuz you mad 'bout some shit I don't even know about!"

"What, you scared? I didn't even attempt to come at you—yet."

"Yet? Bitch, if you tryna jump, then pop off! Ain't nobody scared of ya' ass!"

"You don't have to be scared to get that ass beat!"

I looked past Kitanya to her friend that was obviously looking for trouble. She was steadily creeping in my direction.

"Girl, do you know me?"

The female said, "Should I know you?"

"The way you creepin', you would think you know me. But then again, if you creepin', then you don't know me or how I get down."

"I don't care to know either!"

That was all that was said, before Markel stood to his feet and stood in front of me. Kitanya's eyes went from me to Markel.

"Oh, so you her protector now, instead of her driver?"

"Don't worry 'bout all dat, just worry about you and homegirl backing the fuck up out this yard and making it up the street."

"I'm not goin' nowhere; this ain't cha' business. Move ya' ass to the side!"

"Nah, dat ain't about to happen. I'm not about to stand here and watch y'all bitches jump my girl. I ain't dat type a nigga; dat shit ain't going down. Move back!"

Markel pulled his phone from his jacket pocket and sent someone a text, then he calmly placed his phone back in his pocket. One of the dudes outside the gate said, "Yo, my nigga, mind yo' fuckin' business, before I come up in there and fuck yo' ass up!"

"If you confident, nigga, then do you!"

"You not ready for a nigga like me!"

"Yeah, aight," is all Markel said.

That's went Kitanya darted around him and came charging right at me. The second female tried it, but was snatched back and pushed out of the yard by Markel. Soon as KiKi reached me, she tried to reach out for my hair. I leaned my head back to avoid her hands and swung my left hand at her face, popping her in the mouth. She switched up her tactics, since she wasn't about to be pulling on my hair. She balled up her fist and swung back, and she caught me on the side of my face.

I felt that shit; my face was stinging as her fist connected with it. She tried to follow-up with another connection, but I quickly moved back out the way, then rushed her ass. When I got close enough, I started swinging punches at her, as if I were a professional boxer. That one hit was all she was about to get off me; I didn't give her another chance to swing on me and connect. I kept punching her in her face repeatedly, until she stumbled back and fell down four steps, before reaching the ground. The females standing outside the gate were yelling for Kitanya to get up and beat my ass, while also trying to get past Markel, to get at me for beating Kitanya's ass.

I rushed down the steps, while she tried her best to stand to her feet. I kicked her in the back of her leg, causing her left leg to buckle, bringing her down on one knee. I punched her in her face, drawing blood from her nose and lip.

"AHH, BITCH!" She tried to swing back, but kept missing.

I kept swinging blow-after-blow at her face, and kept connecting with each swing.

"Don't ever bring ya' ass back the fuck over here again! Bitch, I will fuckin' knock ya' damn head off!" I said as I kept connecting my fist to her face.

A red and black car pulled up and double parked in front of my house. Three females and two dudes got out and rushed over towards the gate. One female grabbed the chick that tried to get at me with Kitanya, by her hair and swung her back away from the gate. The two dudes that had come with Kitanya were about to say something, until they saw the two big niggas that were with the females. I figured they were the ones Markel had texted, while he stood between Kitanya, her friend, and me, before the fight even started. When Markel finally turned in my direction, he saw how badly I'd already beaten Kitanya. She was leaking from her nose and mouth, and I'd swelled up her eye. It was swollen shut; she couldn't see shit out of it.

I felt so much anger flowing through my body, that I didn't even want to stop hitting her. Markel grabbed me and quickly pulled me up off her.

"Babe, dat's enough—chill. You got her!"

"Nah, we not done! Let me go!"

"Nah, she good! You done, chill… Relax, Zya! Calm down, Ma."

Markel carried me to the top of the stairs as Kitanya struggled to get up off the ground. She was a little dazed; one of the dudes that was with her had to come in the yard and hold her up. We watched as they slowly moved up the block, until they disappeared. Once they were gone, Markel finally let me go. One of the females smiled and said,

"Damn Kel, dat's ya' girl? She's a savage wit' them hands; I like her."

Even though she was complimenting me, I wasn't in the mood for it. But I chose not to say anything, while trying to calm this raging anger inside of me.

"Yeah yo, this my first time seeing her bang out. She's definitely, a beast wit' them hands. I got me a winner right here. Yo, I'll check y'all later; thanks for looking out. The crowd needed to be tamed." He laughed.

One of the dudes said, "No problem, my nigga. You comin' through, later?"

"Nah, I'm gon' be chillin' wit' my lady, but if y'all niggas need me, then hit my phone."

"Aight, check you later." They gave each other dap and left.

CHAPTER 11

Giving You My All

Zya

Forty-five minutes later

I was still pumped up and angry about the fight with Kitanya. I was even madder, knowing that the friendship Kitanya and I once had was now over. I still don't know what reasons she had to want to fight me, or dislike me. Whatever they were, must've been a good enough reason for her to bring people over to my house to watch her get her ass whipped.

Markel and I were on the porch. He was leaning back against the railing, and I was in front of him, hugging him. I had my face in his chest, letting out tears of anger, while Markel spoke softly in my ear. He was telling me that everything was going to be alright, and that I shouldn't worry too much about being friends with Kitanya.

"If she could bring herself to fight someone she considered to be her best friend, then she really wasn't your friend from jump."

"Yeah, you right. But that doesn't change how I feel about the situation, though. She was something like a sister to me, at least in my eyes. I just can't believe that shit went down like that."

"Can't nobody control her actions, but her. She made that choice, so let it go."

"You right, I'm over it."

Markel wiped the tears from my eyes as I looked up in his face, then he kissed my lips.

"Let's go inside; I'm cold," I said.

Markel laughed, "You wouldn't be cold if you didn't bust out yo' jacket like the *Hulk*, ready to smash on a bitch." I playfully punched him in his chest as I moved back.

"Shut up, fool."

We made our way inside the house, and I told him to have a seat in the living room, while I check on my mother. After closing the door, I went upstairs to my mother's room. I gently pushed the door open and peeked my head inside. My mother quickly turned her head towards the window and started wiping her face.

I walked inside and closed the door behind me. "Mommy, you alright?" I walked closer to the bed and noticed she was wiping tears from her eyes. "Ma…"

I made my way around the bed to my mother's side. When I looked at her, her face was covered in wetness. Seeing my mother in here alone, crying, hurt my heart. She had me ready to cry with her.

"I'm ok, don't worry about me."

"Are you in pain, do you need something to drink? Is it time for you to take your meds?" She looked up at me, and her eyes grew big.

"WHAT THE HELL HAPPENED TO YOUR FACE!" she shouted.

I put my hand over the noticeable bruise on my face, where Kitanya had hit me.

"It's nothing…"

"What the hell you mean, it's nothing? Jaz'Zyazia Chanel Robinson, you have a huge bruise on the side of your face! Tell me what happened! Now!"

"I got into it with Kitanya."

"I thought y'all were friends?"

"I thought so too; but lately, she's been acting funny with me. Especially around Markel. The first time she met him, she started with her mess. I brushed it off at first, but then she tried to pop up over here with her boyfriend, knowing you ain't want him around here."

"Oh, no the hell she didn't, either!"

"Yes, she did. She had some nerve. At first, I thought he was being funny by coming here. I told him he had to go. He asked why, and I told him. He told me Kitanya told him to come. I felt disrespected, so I told her to leave to."

"And?"

"And they left, but after they left, she texted my phone, threatening to see me later when I was alone. I'm always with Markel, so when am I alone, and even if she does catch me by myself, am I supposed to be scared?"

"Hell no, you're a Robinson! You're my child; we don't scare easily."

I giggled at my mother's response; she's too much sometimes.

"Well, she tried it with me not too long ago. She came over here with some of her other friends. I guess they were going to attempt to jump me, but Markel wasn't having it. I was ready for it, though. Kitanya managed to make it around Markel, and she ended up getting one lucky hit off, but she ended up leaving looking tore up."

"That's my girl! You know I don't condone all that fighting and drama shit. But, when a bitch brings that shit to you, once they put hands on you... Whoop dat ass!" my mother said proudly.

We laughed for a bit about the situation, but then I decided to get a little serious with my mother. This would probably be the only chance I get to talk to her about what happened.

"So, Ma, what got you crying?"

"Nothing, just had this crazy dream that left a sour taste in my mouth."

"What was your dream about, was it about what happened to you?"

"Kind of..."

"Why did Shalaine come over here and attack you?"

"I don't know; she just asked for you, claiming she wanted to speak to you about your father and going to California. When I dismissed her, she bugged out on me—that's all."

"I heard from the doctor you were pregnant, and due to the seriousness of the injuries, you lost the baby." My mother didn't say anything, she just quietly turned her head to look out the window. "Is it true, you were still seeing Daddy?" Still, she said nothing. I sat there a little longer, waiting to get an answer. I thought it was only right for her to give me an answer to my questions, but she wasn't tryna do that.

"Ok, fine, I won't ask again." I got up and walked out the room and headed back downstairs to the living room.

When I walked in the living room, my father was there, standing face-to-face with Markel. They weren't saying anything when I walked in the room. They were just standing there, staring in each other's face. I could only see the look on Markel's face, and he wasn't happy to see my father at all.

"What's going on?" I walked over and stood beside Markel. When I looked in my father's face, he looked angry as hell.

"What the fuck this boy doing in my house? Didn't I tell you I don't want you to be around this boy? He's too old for you!"

"Well, that's just too damn bad! Markel is my boyfriend, and my mother already met him and said that it was ok for us to date each other! I'm not too concerned about what you think of us being together. You have no right to be all up in my business; I'm 18, not 12! Remember that. And you don't live here, so this ain't your house!"

"Watch yourself, Zya!"

"You watch yourself, Karl! C'mon, Markel, let's go."

I grabbed Markel's hand, which seemed to piss my father all the way the fuck off. He grabbed my arm and yanked me towards him.

"Lil' girl, you not gon' keep disrespecting me!" He went to slap me, and I tightly closed my eyes, waiting to feel his big, thick ass hand go across my face.

When I didn't feel his hand go across my face, I opened my eyes to see Markel holding my father's hand in the air.

"You her father, but you not about to hit her in front of me, and you not gon' keep disrespecting me, either," he said in a calm tone.

He flung my father's hand away from me, then he grabbed me, and we both walked out the house and went straight next door to his apartment. I couldn't believe it; Markel had stood up to my father. No, he just challenged the shit out of my father, and I'm sure he was feeling a certain kind of way right now. Good thing I was no longer in the house with him. I was glad Markel had stood up to that man. Somebody needed to let him know about himself and about putting hands on me.

Shit, I already had one fight, I didn't need to have another one. Soon as we made it inside Markel's apartment, I plopped down on his sofa. I was exhausted; that fight had me tired as fuck. Like, I really wanted to lay down, get comfortable, and just close my eyes, until I drift off to sleep. I took it upon myself to take my jacket off and kick my sneakers off, then put my feet up on the sofa. I lay down on the sofa and closed my eyes. Markel came and sat down on the edge of the couch beside me.

"You good, babe?"

"Yeah, I'm just tired... All this bullshit going on in my life right now, got me drained."

"What'chu talkin' 'bout? The fight?"

"I'm speaking on the fight with this bitch, my father, and my mother's situation. It's all draining the shit out of me. I tried to talk to my mother about the whole situation dealing with my father and his bitch, and she just shut down on me. She wouldn't even talk to me about it."

"Maybe she's traumatized by the whole situation…"

"Yeah, maybe…"

"Don't stress it. When she's ready to talk, she will…"

"You don't know my mother; once she shuts down, it's over. But this bitch, Kitanya… Ugh, I can't even do it with this bitch. This fight ain't the end of it. I gotta go to school and see this bitch in every class I got. That means I just might not make it to see graduation, due to having to fuck her ass up again."

"Nah, it won't be your fault if something goes down. I'll be taking you to school and picking you up, so ain't shit going down while I'm around."

"Some things may be out of your hands, Markel. You can't stop everything; you see how that bitch just swerved around ya' ass." I laughed. "She looked like the road runner and shit. Leaving dust in her path to get knocked the fuck down on her ass. That shit was just too funny."

"You wild, though. I ain't know your hands were lethal like that. I may call on you to fight my battles from now on."

"HA! You funny; not doing that!" We laughed, and then ended

up in a kissing fight.

Somehow, Markel had this thing with him, where every time he looked in my eyes with those light brown eyes, he seemed to draw me in closer. He made me want him, like I just wanted to give myself to him. I didn't want to give myself to him physically; I want to be a part of this man, wholeheartedly. I wanted to be with him forever and always, the end. Right now, I was struggling to hold it together, while Markel kissed me passionately and deeply. His kiss was so powerful, that this man had me sitting up on the sofa.

I wanted to straddle him, then rip off his clothes and wildly fuck him, until I could feel his dick throbbing inside of me. But, at the thought of being in so much pain and having my pussy stretched out of shape to fit Markel's massive dick inside of me, I pulled back. Our passionate kiss came to a complete halt; my thoughts were scaring the shit out of me. I felt so nervous, that I was damn near ready to go home, until I remembered my father was over there.

"What's wrong?" Markel asked. "Why your body shaking like that, you cold?"

"No, I'm not cold. I'm feeling some type of way right now."

"Tell me, what's wrong?"

"I want to feel you inside of me… Your kisses got me wanting you badly, but I'm scared as hell. Your dick is huge, and my shit is tight as fuck. All I keep thinking about is that pain."

"Don't worry about it; when you're ready, it will happen."

"I'm ready and want it to happen, but I'm scared."

"Scared of what—me? You ain't gotta be scared of me." He had this sly smirk on his face.

"Ain't nobody scared of you, negro. Move ya' ass!" I pushed him off the sofa as he laughed out loud. Markel is the biggest jokester; he is always playing around. But I liked that about him.

"You hungry?"

"Yeah, but not really..."

"I'll be back. I'm 'bout to change out these clothes, then we can order out and watch a movie."

"Sounds good."

Markel walked off to the other room. I was left alone to fantasize about all the things I wanted him to do to me. I had no choice but to let it go, until I felt I was ready. As I was sitting on the sofa waiting for Markel, his doorbell rang. I didn't move; I figured he heard it and would go see who was at his door. The doorbell rang a second time, three minutes later, and I heard footsteps coming up the stairs outside his door. I'm thinking it was somebody for the third floor, but then I remembered...

"There ain't a third floor dummy, so who the fuck is coming up the stairs?"

Minutes later, there was a knock at the door. I didn't move; I waited for Markel to come answer the door, because this wasn't my house. About three knocks later, Markel comes walking through the house towards the door. He looks at me and says, "Why you didn't answer the door?"

"This ain't my house and it's not for me."

"WHO IS IT?" he yelled out, loud enough for the person on the other side of the door to hear.

I wasn't sure if the person on the other side of the door answered back, because I couldn't hear anything. Markel looked through the peephole, then slightly opened the door.

"What's good, what you want?"

"Ilk, why you not tryna let me in?" I heard a female voice say.

I sat up right on the sofa and placed my sneakers back on my feet, because I wasn't feeling a female standing on the other side of the door tryna get in, while I was in the house.

"The fuck you acting like I'm supposed to allow you access to my apartment for? You not my girl!"

"Since when?"

"Since you ain't never been my girl! I haven't spoken to you for like a year and some change, why you here?"

"I came to le—" He interrupted her from speaking.

"It doesn't matter, you gotta go! I'm busy chillin' with my lady, peace out." She quickly stopped him from closing the door.

"Ya' girl? Ain't no way in hell, you got another bitch up in here, and it ain't been no damn year since the last time you seen me. But, as I was tryna tell you… You got a six-month-old son you need to be supporting!"

"Nah, not mine. I don't have no kids and definitely not by you. Wrong nigga!"

"You tryna play dumb cuz you got some bitch up in here."

I got up and walked to the door, because I can't stand to hear people calling me out my name. I grabbed the door and opened it wide, so the female standing out in the hallway could see me.

"May I help you?" She looked me up and down, then laughed, like I'd said something funny.

"No, you may not. I'm in the middle of talking to my child's father, so please excuse yourself."

"No, you're in the middle of being disrespectful to my man and have no business being at his door. We were in the middle of something; you came here interrupting our good mood. That makes this my business. NOW, according to Markel, he doesn't have any kids, and now you're popping up fussing about a kid that's supposed to be his. Do you have a paternity test stating this child is his?"

"No, I—" I put my hand up, stopping her from saying another word.

"Ok, that's all we needed to know. You can excuse yourself; we'll send you a request in the mail, when he's ready to take the child to be tested. Other than that, I shouldn't see your face again at this house, or even on this street. Bye, boo."

I spoke to the rude ass bitch in a very calm manner, so that I could get my point across. And by the look on her face, I think she got the point.

"Look bitch, how about you mind your own damn business! This is between me and Markel."

"We'll see about that; see your way out. Bye!"

I politely closed the door in the bitch's face and locked it. I looked at Markel, while shaking my head. Then I silently walked back in the living room. I didn't even bother to sit down. I turned and looked at him as he walked in the room.

"I know I said that I was gonna have you tell all ya' bitches they were done. But damn, how many bitches do you have? This is becoming way too much baggage for me, Markel."

"I don't have no other females trailing behind me, Zya. This bitch, I been stopped messing around with her like a year—almost two years ago."

"So, why is she saying she gotta kid by you?"

"She's running game, that's all. She's lying; ain't no way in hell I gotta kid with that female, or any other female. I always strap up."

"I don't believe neither one of y'all right about now."

"I wouldn't lie to you, Zya. I'm being truthful. Besides, you know that chick you embarrassed in the park? They're both friends, and more than likely, she sent her over here to do that shit. Last I knew, that bird ain't have no kids, and if she does, it ain't mine."

"Before I even think about losing my virginity to your ass, you need to get that paternity test done. I'm not tryna fuck with you, if you have a crazy baby momma running around. I don't want to have to fuck this bitch up, for real, Markel."

"You know what, that's fine. When I get this shit done, you can be right there. When the results come back, you can be the one to open the envelope." He was mad; he shook his head and walked out the room. He could be mad all he wants. He needed to know that I wasn't playing no games with his ass, or these random bitches that keep popping up.

CHAPTER 12

Back to the Bullshit

Zya

Monday

A week later

Since that night when I walked out of Markel's house, I hadn't gone back. I haven't even bothered to call him, and he hadn't called or texted me either. Until I see some test results, that's exactly how it was gonna to stay. Yes, I was upset with him, because I was tired of seeing all these bitches. I was going through way too much shit to be dealing with Markel's bitches. So, he needs to handle his business or lose me all together—fuck it.

I was trying not to think about him as I got ready for school. I was stressed and ready to go, as I grabbed my bookbag off my bed and made my way downstairs.

"Zyazia, come in the kitchen," I heard my mother yell out.

I was shocked to see that she was up and out of bed this early. She was still healing from her wounds, and her doctor told her to stay in bed. I walked in the kitchen to see my mother standing at the stove, cooking. "Ma..."

"Your food is on the table; eat quickly before you miss your bus."

"What're you doing out of bed?"

"I'm not handicap. I can move around ya' know."

"I see; excuse me for being just a little concerned."

"Just eat, then take your ass to school." Look who woke up on the wrong side of bed this morning.

My mother's early morning stank attitude seemed to be an everyday thing, since my father showed his face that day. I don't know what they chatted about. I just know she's had a fucked up attitude since then, and she's driving me crazy. I ate and left the house. When I got outside, Markel was standing by his truck. I walked down the stairs and out my gate. I attempted to walk past his ass, towards my bus stop. As I was about to pass him, he reached out and grabbed my arm, then pulled me close.

"You were gonna walk right by a nigga, huh?"

"No, I was going to say hi as I passed you by. I wasn't gonna be that rude, but I need to get to my bus."

"Get in the truck."

"No, I think I'm gonna take the bus to school today."

"And tomorrow?"

"Yeah, maybe tomorrow too."

"Zya, get in the truck; I'll take you to school. C'mon, you're going to be late." I gritted my teeth, then got in the truck. I peeped the smile on his face as I got in. He hurried around the truck to the driver's side, got in, and pulled off from the curb up the block.

As Markel drove me to school, he tried to make conversation by telling me how he's been missing me, and a bunch of other stuff that I wasn't tryna hear. I didn't say one word in response to anything he was saying. When he noticed he was having a one-sided conversation, he stopped talking altogether. When we finally made it to my school, he pulled up to the gate's entrance.

Before I got out, he said, "Zya, I'll be right here waiting for you after school. Don't try to walk right by me, cuz I'll get out and do some funny shit to embarrass you."

"What could you possibly do, that would embarrass me, Markel?"

"I'll get out with nothing but my boxers and socks on and run up on you. I'll act crazy, like a stalker or some shit."

I laughed, "I think you'll be the only one embarrassed, if you do that."

"For real though, Zya. I'll be right here waiting for you. We have an appointment at three that we can't be late for."

"What appointment? What're talking about?"

"I'll see you after school; call me if anything pops off."

I said nothing. I just got out the truck and made my way inside the building. I looked around and didn't see Millian as I made my way to my locker. I grabbed a few books out my locker, and as soon as I closed the door, I saw Millian standing there with her back against the locker that was right next to mine.

"Oh shit, girl! Don't do that, you scared the shit out of me."

"So, um… KiKi won't be coming to school today," she mentioned.

"And you're telling me because, what?"

"Because you fucked her up pretty bad."

"Again, why are you telling me this for?"

"Damn, really Zya? Are you gonna keep pretending like you don't give a shit? That's ya' girl, ya' fuckin' sister!" Millian raised her tone a little above normal.

"First off, don't yell at me. There's no reason for you to be getting loud. I couldn't care less about what's goin' on with Kitanya. She got what she deserved after coming to my house with all them damn people, tryna jump somebody. As for her being my girl, my so-called sister, that's a wrap! There is nothing holding our friendship together, it's over. Since you seem so concerned, after already knowing she threw threats my way, you can walk away from me now and keep your friendship with her. You can't have us both as friends."

"Zya, do you hear yourself? You want me to choose between the two of you? That's fucked up! I can be friends with both of you; I'm not choosing sides or who I'm gonna be friends with. So you can cut this shit out right now. I just wanted you to know how bad you fucked her up, and what you did wasn't right. You both could have sat down and talked about whatever issues you were having with each other."

"You already knew I had no issues with her! So I'm not understanding why you're standing in front of me right now, saying all of this. It's cool, you saw the busted lip and swollen black eye. So what? If the bruises look worse than what they looked when the fight first took place, that's not on me; that's on her for initiating the whole fight."

The bell rang and I walked away, leaving Millian stand by the lockers to collect her thoughts. I went to my first period class and sat in my seat, which was in the center of the room. I didn't care for the shit Millian was saying about Kitanya. Yeah, I beat her ass, blacked her eye, and busted her lip. But there was no way in hell I'd beat her ass to the point that the bitch was crippled. So, why was Millian coming at me like I'd shot the bitch in the face or something?

Millian was doing too much. I'm not understanding why she's coming at me like that, when she already knows how Kitanya was threatening me. She already knew Kitanya was acting funny way before that fight even happened. But it's fine, I got no problem with dismissing my friendship with Millian too. She was acting funny now too, and I couldn't understand why. At this point, I didn't care either.

The day seemed to be moving slower than usual, but once that last bell of the day sounded off, I exited seventh period and headed straight out the building. I had homework in damn near every class. I had two tests to study for this week and wasn't looking forward to doing so. I was in a daze as I walked towards the gate to exit the school yard. I had so much on my mind, I was walking with my head down, deeply lost in my thoughts. I heard Millian calling me from behind, but I had blocked her out.

A few minutes later, Markel's voice could be heard calling out my name too.

"Zya—ZYA LOOK OUT!" Markel yelled out.

When I looked in the direction his voice was coming from, I

saw that he was running in my direction. I looked back to see Millian running my way too, so I looked forward. I saw the same two girls that was at my house with Kitanya. This time, they were with like five other females and two dudes. The group of girls came rushing at me. I quickly dropped my bookbag and got ready for these bitches that were coming at me.

The first female ran up on me. "Yeah bitch, what's up now!" She sprayed me in my eyes with mace. I screamed out, while grabbing at my eyes.

"FUCK!"

"NO, ZYA!" I heard Millian yell out in the distance.

I felt a fist go across my face, then someone kicked the shit out of me. I tried to take a deep breath, but due to the strong smell of the mace, I couldn't breathe easy. When I felt someone grab my hair from behind, I tried my best to pull myself together. I swung around while balling my fist and started going in. I felt my fist connecting with whoever was surrounding me. By then, a crowd had formed. I heard people yelling out random shit.

One person said, "*Damn yo, she got maced and still beating them bitch's ass!*"

Someone else was like, "*Oh, shit! Two more fights popping off. Those niggas tryna jump that dude, look!*"

That's when I heard a female say, "*Oh, hell nah, that's my cousin, Kel! What the fuck is he doing here? I'm 'bouta make a call!*"

Then there was a crowd of females saying, "*Beat that bitch ass, Millian. Get those bitches! Oh shit, ain't that Kitanya?*"

What the fuck was Kitanya doing here? I couldn't see worth a shit; I didn't know what the fuck was going on, but I wasn't tryna stop swinging. Someone grabbed me away from the females.

"Chill out, calm down. It's me!" It was Millian. "Open your eyes," she demanded.

I tried to open my eyes as wide as I possibly could. She poured a bottle of water in my eyes to wash some of the strong chemicals out. When the burning sensation died down a little, and my vision became a bit clearer, I saw KiKi fighting two of the girls that were with her friends. Off to the side, Markel was beating the shit out of one of the two dudes that came with the females. Where the other dude disappeared to, I don't know.

But Millian and I rushed over to the other females, who were tryna sneak up behind Kitanya. Millian and I both snatched them bitches by their hair and yanked them backwards, causing them to hit the ground hard. We started stomping them bitches in the face. I yelled out, "YOU BITCHES WANTED TO RUN UP ON ME AND MACE ME, RIGHT! FUCK YOU! YOU GOT THE WRONG BITCH!"

A few minutes later, Markel made it over to me and grabbed me off the females. But then, school security and the principal came rushing over. Security grabbed the females off the ground, and the principal grabbed me from Markel. He was about to start wilding out, but instead I gave him a look, telling him to chill. I snatched my arm away from Ms. Bragoli and said, "I can walk on my own. I ain't going nowhere." Millian and Kitanya were right there by my side.

I was still puzzled to see Kitanya's face. She had new bruises on her face, two black eyes, and a cut going up the side of her face. What the fuck done happened to her? We were escorted back inside the school to the main office, and the cops were called because these females didn't attend our school. They were trespassing on school property. When we made it in the office, I looked around to see Markel standing off to the side by the door.

Millian, Kitanya, and I were escorted inside the principal's office. We were asked a thousand questions, and we all answered to the best of our ability. When Ms. Bragoli started questioning Kitanya about the scratches and bruises on her face, she said, "Those same females came to my house a few hours earlier and jumped me. They mentioned that they were coming here to fight my friends. I don't know why, but Millian and Zyazia don't know them. I came here to let them know, so they could avoid the fight. But, when I got here it was too late; the fight had already started. I saw the two males jumping Zyazia's boyfriend, and Millian was trying to help Zya. I wasn't about to stand around while these girls were jumping my friends."

Ms. Bragoli said, "Alright, I'll let you girls off with a warning. I don't want to kick you out of school with graduation being only two months away. But, if you get into any trouble from now until then, that's it. You girls won't graduate, got it!" We silently shook our heads, while Ms. Bragoli continued to talk. "I will have to call your parents to alert them on the current situation, but you girls are free to go. Be safe, and no more fighting."

We walked past the small group of females, and they started throwing threats towards Kitanya. KiKi walked right on by without saying nothing, like she was scared. All that shit she said to me, but she kept quiet and didn't say one word to them. I bit my tongue and didn't say anything either, since we were still in the school. I grabbed Markel's hand and walked out the office and the school altogether. When we got outside, I yanked Markel's arm back, making him come to a complete stop. I grabbed his face with both hands and examined it. This negro didn't have not one scratch on him.

He looked in my face and said, "Your eyes are red as fuck. You wanna go by the emergency room and get your eyes checked?"

"No, just drop me off at home. No wait, didn't you say you wanted me to go somewhere with you?"

"Nah, I'm gonna drop you off home and go do what I needed to do. I'll just get back up with you right after."

No other words were exchanged between Markel and I, but when I turned and looked at Kitanya, it was another story.

"I thought you had an issue with me. Why would you come all the way here to fight for me?"

"There's more to the story that you don't know... We may have our issues, but I wasn't about to let that shit go down like that."

"First off, I've never had an issue with you. You're the one with all the issues, remember that. You came to my house to fight me; it wasn't the other way around."

"True, and I apologize for that; I took things too far. I was jealous of the relationship you have with Markel. In my head, I compared your relationship with my own. And no, I didn't bring Jeff over to your house on purpose. He insisted on coming after we had a whole argument about him not going. I wanted to go, because I didn't want to be around his ass. But, he flipped shit and put it on me."

"So, why didn't you deny it? Did you think I would've believed him over you?"

"No, before I met up with Millian, he'd already choked me out at my house. So, I wasn't tryna get into it with him in front of y'all."

"We already know he be hitting on you. We can tell, but why you never spoke out and said something to us, personally? You make it look like you love that shit… So, we stay out of your shit with him, cuz he's ya' man. But damn, you're taking your shit out on me, and that's not cool."

Kitanya started crying; she just broke completely down. I felt so bad for her. Millian and I rushed to her side and wrapped our arms around her.

"KiKi, stop crying. Please, don't let this shit get you down like this. We'll handle this shit together," Millian said.

"C'mon, Markel has somewhere to be, so he's gonna drop us off at my house."

We all walked out the school yard to the truck. Millian got in the backseat with Kitanya, when Markel and I got in the truck, then we left the area, heading for my house. The way Markel was driving, it didn't take us long to pull up in front of my house. I kissed him, then exited the truck and made my way in the house, with Millian and Kitanya following right behind me. My mother was standing in the hallway by the door, waiting for me. Ms. Bragoli must've called my mother as soon as we walked out her office.

My mother looked angry as hell, but I didn't care. The fight wasn't my fault; those girls came to me. I told Millian to take Kitanya up to my room and close the door. My mother turned and walked into the living room, where my father was sitting on the sofa.

"What's he doing here?"

"Your principal called me," he said.

I rolled my eyes and took a seat on the sofa, since he was sitting in the chair. My mother also sat down. The first thing she said when she opened her mouth was, "What's Kitanya doing in my house, especially after the fight you two had?"

"She's here because she and I have some things to talk about."

My father said, "What happened at school today, who were the ones that jumped you after school?"

"I don't know who the girls were. But I plan to find out, when I talk to Kitanya."

"Tell her to come down," my father said. Why the fuck was he minding my business again, anyways?

"No, I'm not doing that. I'll be talking to her on my own; besides, I don't need you in my business like that."

"Where was that nigga you're dealing with, while you were getting jumped?"

"He was there too…"

"Doing what, nothing?"

"If you must know, he got jumped by two dudes, trying to help me. So, you can stop worrying about Markel; he's not your concern!"

"You're my child, so he is my concern."

"You keep telling yourself that to make yourself feel better..."

"Jaz'Zyazia..."

I stood from the sofa. "Stay out of my business and worry about your damn self. I'm old enough to take care of myself. I don't need a father like you; you should worry about the baby that y'all have been tryna keep secret, that no longer exists, thanks to your bitch!"

I walked out of the living room and up to my bedroom. I slammed the door and locked it, to keep my parents out of my room. I turned on my music to calm the anger I was feeling. It took a while, but when I finally calmed down, I turned off the music. Kitanya, Millian, and I sat on my bed and had a long talk about Kitanya's friends, her relationship with Jeff, and what's been going on with her. Millian and I learned a lot about the type of life KiKi has been living, when she's not around us. Shit was crazy; she said since day one of getting with Jeff, he's been beating her ass.

When she tries to leave him, shit gets worse, so she chose to stay. Her only parent living was her mother. Kitanya told us that she was strung out on crack, and her little brother Jaqaun was staying with her grandparents in North Philly. She was too old to move in with them, so she continued to stay with her mother. She went on to tell us that one of the females that fought me is messing around with Jeff. He treats the girl way better than what he treats KiKi.

All I could say to her for the moment was, "Don't worry about that nigga. I'll talk to my mother and see what I can do." Even Millian said she would see if her parents would let Kitanya stay with them. I would probably have to get in a good enough place with my father to see what he could do as an attorney, to get Kitanya out of her mother's house and away from Jeff.

CHAPTER 13

Coming Together, One Happy Family

Marsha

Later that night...

$\mathcal{O}$nce Zya's friends left the house, Karl and I went upstairs to speak to her. Zya's door was locked, for reasons unknown. I've never had a problem with Zya locking her door before, because she's never locked it before. She must be upset with me and her father, but we needed to have this talk. It was important for us to have this talk, because Karl and I were talking about possibly getting back together. We haven't gotten a divorce as of yet, and weren't really planning to get one anytime soon.

I didn't want to get back with my husband and allow him to come back into the house, while his relationship with Zya was falling apart. I wasn't trying to play referee every single day with them. I would've never imagined Zya and her father's relationship would ever get this bad. She was always Daddy's lil' girl. He would buy her anything she ever wanted. Now, she didn't want to have anything to do with the man.

I was left stuck in the middle of my husband and daughter's mess. This was hard for me to handle, because I was still very much in love with the man I've been with damn near all my life. It's not like he's been abusing her or anything, so why was she taking this thing with her father so far? I didn't understand it, but we were going to work this mess out.

Before knocking on Zya's door, I looked up in my husband's face. "Karl, if she does open the door to let us in, don't go in here acting a fool and talking shit. A lot has changed since you've been gone. Zya is right; she's old enough to live her own life without you butting in and telling her what to do."

"So, what? Am I supposed to stand around and allow her to do as she pleases and talk to me however she feels?"

"Wasn't it you who taught her in order to get respect, you got to give respect? Well, it's time to practice what you preach."

"Yeah, ok…"

"I'm serious, and if you're not going to respect her and stay out of her personal business, then there is no purpose of you stepping foot back in this house." I paused to allow my words to sink in, then I continued speaking truth into this man's ears. "You haven't been acting much like her father, you've been acting like a possessive boyfriend. You were once her protector, now I don't know what you are. You're the real reason things in this house have changed so much. It's time you face those facts."

"I don't know what you're talking about."

"Well, keep not knowing then…"

I knocked on Zyazia's door and waited for her to answer. I knocked a second time, and that's when I heard movement. Seconds later, Zya opened the door—looked out—then walked away without opening the door any further. I pushed the door open just in time to see her walk over to her desk and sit down. She had several textbooks open, along with two or three different notebooks, taking notes.

"Are you busy? Your father and I would like to talk to you."

"Yes Mother, I'm very busy right now. I have tests to study for. Did you cook anything? I only opened the door because I thought you were bringing me some food."

"No, I haven't started cooking yet. We wanted to talk to you first. Can you give us about twenty minutes of your time, please?"

She pushed the button to light up the screen on her phone, then looked back at me.

"I don't really have twenty minutes, so I'll give y'all about ten minutes. I have a math test tomorrow; if I fail, it'll be both your faults."

I sat down on the bed, closest to where Zya was. Karl chose to stand, so I started telling Zya about everything that me and Karl talked about earlier.

"Zya, your father is going to move back in, and we're going to try to put our family back together."

"What?" She looked at her father, and she rolled her eyes at him

147

as she looked me in my eyes. "After everything that happened, you're willing to take him back? Wow, you must've lost your mind…"

"I think both you and your father should talk and work out your differences."

"Work out our differences? There's nothing to work out. The problem is, he cheated and y'all kept messing around with each other, secretly. You got pregnant and didn't even mention any of that to me. I had to find out through a doctor that saved your life, after you were stabbed by his ugly ass girlfriend. Now you expect me to play nice with this guy that I no longer know?"

"Zya, he's still your father. All that disrespectful shit, and you cursing at him, is going to stop! You still live in my house—our house— and we're still your parents!"

She shook her head with a disappointed look on her face.

"That's good to know. I don't have no problem with moving out your house. That way, you can live a happy life with your husband, Mother. You won't have to worry about me being disrespectful to a man that disrespected both of us. I don't see how you can allow yourself to put up with this mess. Whelp, I'm not you… I don't have to put up with it."

I was shocked to hear Zyazia speaking to me like this; she was making me upset. No, she was pissing me off to the point that I was ready to slap the shit out of her. Luckily for her, she'd gone through enough shit these last couple days. That was the only thing stopping me from slapping the color off her face.

"Look—" She cut in.

"Sorry Mother, I have studying to do. I can't keep talking about this all night. Maybe you and your husband can finish this conversation in the privacy of your own room..." She turned away from me and started reading her textbook and taking notes.

I sat there dumbfounded, while looking at the back of her head. I wanted to say something to her, but chose not to. Instead, I just got up and walked out the room with her father following right behind me. When we walked out the room, I closed the door behind us, leaving her to do her studying. There was nothing else to be said, because she wasn't going to listen. She would rather move out of the house than have her father back.

I couldn't blame her for the way she felt. She was right; her father did do us wrong by cheating with the next chick. But, I was willing to forgive and forget to put my family back together. I wanted us all to live a happy life, without all the complications. Maybe I was asking for too much. Maybe I was wasting my time. Maybe I should've died in the operating room along with my unborn child. If things were going to continue down the fucked up path they were going down, why would God spare my life and bring me back to this bullshit? Or maybe Jaz'Zyazia was right... Maybe it was time for her to move out and be on her own. I can open her a bank account and put enough money in it to start her off. She wasn't a little girl anymore; she could move out and live her own life.

I wasn't ready to be without my husband in my life just yet. I wasn't trying to be some old, lonely hag, regretting my own decisions. That wasn't going to me, but even if I did allow Karl to come back in this house and in my life, a lot of shit will change, whether he likes it or not. He'll start living by my rules, not his own, and if he continued to cheat, then I would have to teach him a lesson of my own.

~VENOMOUS~

Zya

After kicking my parents out of my room, it became challenging to focus on my studies. The only thing that kept running through my head, was my mother telling me that my father was moving back in the house. She must love it when he cheats on her with random females. Like, why would she take him back after being attacked and almost killed by Shalaine's crazy ass? What do she think is gonna happen, when Shalaine finds out they're getting back together? I don't think I can handle the type of drama that's about to go down between these old heads.

I can't stand to see my mother getting fucked up over a man that keeps cheating on her. She must have low self-esteem. It's either that, or she's just desperate and insecure. He's my father, but damn, my mother can do better. I planned on getting a job when I graduate and move out, but I doubt that I'll be able to wait that long. Not with my father moving back in the house.

I couldn't stand being around him or seeing his face for too long. I got up from my desk after closing my books; I was done studying for today. I slid my feet in my sneakers and grabbed my jacket. I reached under my mattress, where I always kept money hidden in an envelope. I grabbed the envelope and took $40 out, then slid the envelope back under my mattress. I was starving and wasn't in the mood to wait around for my mother to decide when she was ready to cook.

Since her husband was back, I'm sure all she was worried about was being up under his ass, anyways. I grabbed my jacket and left the house. Upon leaving out the house, I spotted Markel's Benz truck. I thought about going to his house to see what he was up to, but decided against it. Instead, I walked up the block towards the pizza place. I was too hungry to think about doing anything else, or being around anyone.

My stomach was growling, telling me to put a little pep in my step. I got halfway up the block, when I heard my name being called. When I turned around, I saw Markel walking in my direction. I stood there waiting for him to catch up. When he finally made it over to where I was standing, we started walking together.

"Where are we going?" he asked.

"To the pizza place; I'm starving. Hey, do you mind if I crash at your place tonight?"

"Huh? Your mom ain't gon' allow you to stay over at my house..."

"Markel, I'm not a little girl. My mother can't tell me what to do and where to go. We're not agreeing on some things, and I just don't want to be in the same house with her. I'm thinking about moving out anyways."

"Moving out? You want to move in with me?"

"Um, no. You live directly next door to my house... Why would I want to move in with you and still gotta see my parents every day? I'm not doing that..."

"We can find a new place to move in together, if we choose to move in with each other. I don't have a problem with that."

"I have to get a job before I think about moving anywhere with anyone."

"Don't worry about all that, I got'chu."

"Yeah, and you got these randoms popping up too."

"I don't have no one popping up; stop worrying about other people and just focus on us. How about that?"

"Alright, fine…" I didn't say another word as we continued our short journey to the pizza place. I hope I was making the right decision with Markel. We haven't been together that long, and now we were talking about moving in together. I hope I don't end up regretting this move I was about to make.

~VENOMOUS~

Thirty minutes later

After picking up a half-cheese, half-bacon pizza, Markel walked me back to my house to pick up some clothes, my toothbrush, and an extra pair of sneakers for school tomorrow. I didn't bother to speak to my parents, as I walked right back out the door. Markel and I went straight up to his apartment. He cut on a movie as I washed my hands in his bathroom sink. When I got back in the living room, he had two tall glasses and a bottle of Sprite that hadn't even been cracked open yet. We ate pizza, while watching an old movie. We were watching *Warriors,* one of my favorite old school movies besides *Grease,* starring John Travolta.

When we were done eating pizza, I wiped my hands and mouth on a napkin, and then leaned my head on Markel's shoulder. After eating four slices of pizza, I was tired.

"Bae, can you give me a cloth and a towel. I want to jump in the shower real quick, before I get too tired to do it later."

Once he gave me what I needed, I went into the bathroom and ran the shower. I got undressed, then walked over to the mirror and pulled my hair up in a high ponytail, then got in the shower. I stood under the steaming hot water raining down from the wide showerhead. After a few minutes of enjoying the heat from the water caressing my body, I lathered the soap on the washcloths and began scrubbing the stress of the day from my body. When I was sure I scrubbed every inch of my body, I rinsed away the soap , then cut the water off.

Before stepping out of the shower, I reached for the towel, then wrapped it around my body. When I stepped out, I grabbed another towel that Markel had left in the bathroom for me and dried the rest of my body. I walked out of the bathroom and went straight to Markel's room; he was still in the living room watching the movie. I saw that he'd left me one of his wife-beaters on his bed. It was folded neatly, waiting for me to put it on. This was going to be a little weird, because I didn't like to sleep with panties or a bra on.

Oh well, I had to be comfortable when I slept. I put the beater on and walked over to Markel's dresser and saw that he had my favorite Shea Butter lotion. I loved the smell of it; I had everything from the lotion to the hair products in my room on my dresser. I knew Markel and I had a few things in common; he used Shea lotion just like me. Anyways, I rubbed lotion on my body and when I was done, I laid across Markel's bed and fell asleep. It was still fairly early. It had to have been a little before eight thirty. I didn't care; I was too tired to hold my eyes open. I wanted tonight to be the night I give him my goodies, but shit, once my head hit the pillow, I was knocked out cold.

CHAPTER 14

Love All Over Me

Zya

*I*t's been a week already, and I've been staying with Markel the entire time. I went home last Friday to get some of my things and ended up getting into a heated argument with my father. He claimed that he didn't approve of me slowly moving my things into Markel's apartment. All I said to him was, *"That's a problem that you will have to deal with alone."* I haven't seen my father since then. My mother be texting my phone here and there, but we don't speak much anymore either.

Markel gave me a key to his apartment, making me feel all special and shit. Every other night we go out on dates; like, to the movies, out to eat, and sometimes we chill with some of his friends too. He introduced me to his only sister, Kim, short for Kimberly. She's real cool; she acts like a female Markel—she got jokes for days. Their bond is tight as hell. They made me wish I wasn't an only child, but I had no siblings to hold me down and joke around with.

Millian and Kitanya were the only ones I had around me that were like sisters to me. Other than that, I was alone—good thing I have Markel in my life now. Every day, he'd take me to school, pick me up, and even help me study. When it was just us, alone, we would talk about me going to college and wanting to work. He often asked me about my future and what plans I had lined up for myself. Right now, my future was unclear.

I didn't know if I want to go to college right after high school, or if I wanted to take a year off. I guess I'll figure it all out in due time. Right now, the only thing I was worried about was not burning this chicken I was frying on the stove. I was growing tired of eating out almost every day, so I had Markel pick up some groceries at the supermarket. For the last 20 minutes, I've been cooking for the both of us. Fried chicken, mashed potatoes with gravy, and no, these potatoes aren't from the box.

I also made corn and French cut string beans mixed together, corn bread, and biscuits. I even made strawberry-kiwi kool-aid, something I haven't had since I was little. When I was done cooking, I cleaned up my mess and made Markel a plate, as well as a plate for myself. I don't know why he had a table in the kitchen, because we never ate at the table once. When I walked in the living room, I told him he had to go pour us some kool-aid because my hands were full. He did as I asked and came back in the living room carrying two tall cups of kool-aid.

He sat the cups on the table, then grabbed his plate. I waited for him to say my food was nasty, but he didn't. He started eating everything on his plate, so I started eating too. When we were done, he smiled at me.

"Damn babe, you can throw hands and you can cook. That's a plus."

"Whatever, fool. What does knowing how to fight gotta do with knowing how to cook?"

"Nothing, it's just good that you know how to do both. Now I know if needed, you got my back, and that I won't starve to death."

We laughed "You so stupid, Markel."

After we were done eating, Markel took everything back in the kitchen. I could hear the water running in the sink, so I knew he was washing the dishes. I got up and walked in the kitchen; I walked up behind him, wearing only a long V-neck t-shirt, nothing else. I wrapped my arms around his waist. Without looking back at me he said, "Aye, what's up, Ma?"

"I just thought about how much I appreciate you." He cut the water off in the sink and turned around, pulling me into his embrace as he leaned back on the sink.

"I appreciate you too, Zya. If it weren't for you, I would still be in them streets hustling harder than ever and doing some crazy shit. Instead, I'm here with you enjoying our time together."

"I hope this time never ends…"

"I feel the same way," he said, then lowered his head and kissed my lips.

"Markel, I love you."

"Love you too, Ma."

We stood there wrapped up in each other's arms, kissing. I felt my body heating up all over. A few minutes later, I found myself telling Markel to make love to me. He picked me up in his arms, and he had me straddling him in mid-air, as he continued to kiss my lips and navigate his way over to the table. He slowly laid me down on the table, while still passionately kissing my lips. I felt my juices begin to flow; I couldn't hold back. I sat up on the table and pulled his shirt over his head, then began unbuckling his belt.

"You sure this is what you want? You ready for this," he asked.

I silently shook my head. I was scared to death, but I wanted to be brave enough to allow myself to receive the man I was falling head over heels in love with. Once I freed him of his belt and unfastened his jeans, I pulled them down along with his boxers, freeing his massive anaconda. That's exactly what his big ass dick reminded me of, a large anaconda snake. It looked hungry as it stood at attention, ready and waiting to devour me.

"Just be gentle with me; don't hurt me."

He kissed me, then said, "Don't worry, I got'chu."

Our lips connected and our tongues dances to an unheard beat of its own. Markel stroked his dick, then slid it up and down my clit, sending me into a frenzy. All I could do was moan out as I bit down on my lip. Then he slowly slid his large mushroom head inside of my wetness.

"OOH! SSssh," is all that could be heard escaping my lips, as I closed my eyes and wrapped my arms around Markel's neck.

"You good?" I shook my head in an up and down motion.

"Keep going…" He pushed a couple more inches deeper inside of me, then he went deeper until all 10 inches was balls deep. "Oh, my fuckin' goodness. Shit!"

His dick was so big, that my pussy felt like it was hugging his shaft like a tight pair of gloves on a fat hand. He began moving in and out of me slowly, until the pain became pleasure, and I'd released my tight grip from around his neck. I placed my hands around his waist pulling him deeper inside of me.

"Mmm… Ooo…" I moaned.

"Shit! You got me about to nut already; yo' pussy is so damn tight," he said, then I felt his dick throbbing inside of me.

But, he wasn't finished yet. Markel picked me up and carried me to the bedroom, then laid me across the bed. He had me turn on my side as he stepped out of his pants and lay beside me. He grabbed my leg and raised it high in the air, then inserted his dick inside me once again. "Damn…" is all Markel kept saying every other minute, sounding like he was struggling to maintain his composure.

Markel pushed his manhood deep inside of me, while still holding my leg up as I lay on my side, grabbing at the sheets. "OH, FUCK! FUCK—FUCK, SHIT!" I screamed out so loud, I'm sure his neighbors could hear me. "I'm 'bouta cum… Ooh—I'm cumm—I'm cumming baby!" I juiced all over his big ass dick. Not long after, his dick was throbbing inside of me, once again. I could feel him filling me up with seeds, that's when I realized he hadn't strapped up.

I needed to get my ass up and take a quick shower, but my pelvis was hurting like hell and my pussy was sore.

"I'm about to take a shower, wanna get in with me?" Markel asked.

"No, I'm good. I'll get in after you. I need time to collect my thoughts and gain some damn energy back."

He didn't say anything, he just laughed as he got out the bed naked, heading out the room towards the bathroom. I balled up in the fetal position and grabbed at my pussy as if I had a dick. Why does the first time got to be so damn painful, but feel so good at the same time? It doesn't help that Markel's dick is thick and long. It's all good; I just hope my pussy can get used to being fucked by such a big ass dick. Once Markel got out the shower, I got in. I was still hurting, but I tried my best not to show it.

When I got out the shower, I was expecting to walk back in the room, get in the bed, and cuddle up with Markel. But, when I got back in the room, Markel was gone. Instead, there was a sealed envelope on the pillow with another folded paper on top of it. I sat down on the bed and grabbed the top paper first, it said:

Hey Babe,

I had to run out real quick. I got an important call; I'll be back real soon though. So, don't worry about nothing. By the time you wake up in the morning, I will already be laying by your side. Hope that cootie not too sore. If so, I'll kiss it and make it better. Smiley face. In the meantime, open the envelope and tell me what's up. I haven't looked at it yet, like I promised before, I wanted you to be the first to see it. Hit me up when you read it.

Love,

Markel

I looked over at the envelope and saw it was from the health department on the east-side. "Could this be the paternity test results?" I said out loud. I grabbed the envelope and opened it. I read the paper carefully, word-for-word. It said: *Markel Spencer, it is proven 99.999 percentage that you are not the father of Mark Jennings.* I'm guessing Mark Jennings is the girl's baby's name. That's crazy. Did she go as far as to name her child after Markel to make her story believable? Bitches will do anything to mess up a nigga's life. What the fuck be wrong with these hoes?

I never doubted Markel when he said that he wasn't that baby's father. But, he still had to prove himself. I didn't want anything or anyone coming in between us, and that's what his groupies were trying so hard to do. They were all so used to messing around with him, that they just don't want to let him go. Well fuck it, I'll stand by his side and fight for what's mine. Markel Spencer belongs to me.

~VENOMOUS~

Graduation Day

June fifteenth

Yess, the day has finally come for me, Kitanya, and Millian to walk across the stage and receive our diplomas. I was happy that school was about to finally be over and done with. I hadn't applied to any colleges and wasn't sure if I planned to do so at all. Maybe I'll settle for going to a community college, like Housatonic, or I can just apply to the University of Bridgeport. My bakery teacher said upon completion of school, I'd be able to start working at a bakery that works with the school's trade department. But I won't know which bakery until I walk across the stage and receive my certificate of completion for bakery.

In my head, I'm telling myself that I'll end up fat as hell working at somebody's bakery. But fuck it, it's a job; I wasn't about to start complaining about getting a job straight out of school. At least I wouldn't have to be working at McDonald's or Burger King. We were let out of school early to prepare for tonight. Our graduation ceremony was being held at the Klein Memorial Theatre. The theatre itself was big, but it was nice.

Kitanya and Millian went home to get ready, then they would be coming over to Markel's house when they were done. By the time they'd gotten here, I was already dressed in a high-low, pale pink, sequined, strapless chiffon dress that came down to my mid-thigh. It was beautiful; it was embedded with diamonds from the middle of the sweetheart neckline, trailing down towards the bottom of my abdomen. I wore diamond embedded, sequined, round-toe decorated platform shoes with the diamond tassels. Markel had picked out my whole outfit, but I picked out my shoes. My hair was in medium-sized curls, hanging low, down my back.

The evening before, I'd gotten my nails done at the nail salon downtown, so I wouldn't have to rush to get them down today. Since I still wasn't on good terms with my parents, I thought about not giving them tickets to come to my graduation. But then, I decided to put all the petty bullshit aside and slid an envelope in the mailbox two nights ago with two tickets for both my parents, so they wouldn't miss this proud moment. After all, I was their only child. I wouldn't want them to miss out on seeing me walk the stage to receive my diploma. It was on them now, if they wanted to take the invitation and attend my graduation.

I was in the bathroom doing my makeup, when I heard Markel's doorbell ring. I didn't even hear when Markel walked out the house to answer the downstairs door. I just heard when he came back upstairs and closed the door. Markel walked into the bathroom; I was finished doing my makeup and was about to walk out the bathroom, when I saw Markel.

He looked at me from head-to-toe, "Damn babe, you're looking real sexy in that dress. But um, your parents are here to see you, and your girls are here too. We'll wait for you outside at the truck."

I silently shook my head, then turned back around to look at myself in the mirror. Markel walked out the bathroom as I started to take in a few deep breaths and exhale. I wasn't trying to get into it with my parents, so hopefully, they weren't here to start no shit. I walked out the bathroom, down the small hallway, and into the living room to see my parents sitting on the sofa. When I walked in the room, they both stood to their feet. My mother instantly covered her mouth as tears started to flow down her face.

My father looked at me with a glimpse of happiness in his eyes.

"Oh, my god… Sweetheart, you look so beautiful. You look like a princess in that dress, wow!" my mother said, full of excitement.

"Thank you," I said as my mother rushed over and hugged me.

"Who did your hair? Did you get it done at the salon?" she asked.

"No, I did it myself."

"Wow, looks like it was done by a professional stylist. Maybe you should've taken up hairdressing instead of bakery."

"Yeah, maybe... I love cooking, though. Are you accepting my invitation to my graduation?" I asked.

"You know we wouldn't miss it. Of course we're going. We wanted to get some pictures with you and the girls and Markel too. He looks handsome today."

"Thanks, Mom."

I looked over at my father, his face went from looking happy to sad. I wasn't sure of the thoughts that were going through his head, but I'm sure I was about to find out. He looked like he had so much to say.

"Dad, I—."

He put his hand up, stopping me from saying what I was about to say.

"After talking to your mother, I've realized that I've been being a jerk. I want to apologize to you, and I'll also apologize to your boyfriend too. It breaks my heart to see that the closeness we once had—that father/daughter bond that once held us together—is gone."

"Daddy, please..."

"Zya, I should've never hurt you and your mother. Because of the problems your mother and I were having, I cheated, and I was wrong. It won't happen again. I wanted to tell you all this time that after finding out about what happened to your mother, I'd stopped dealing with Shalaine's crazy ass. I just want to get back what we all once had. I want us all to be a family again."

My father had me about to cry, but I fought to hold my composure.

I couldn't allow myself to cry and mess up my makeup. I walked over to my father and wrapped my arms around him.

"That bond we once had, will always be there, Daddy. You just have to loosen up your grip on me; I'm not a little kid anymore."

"You're right, but could you at least move back into the house?"

"Nope, I like it better here with Markel. The good thing about being here is, I don't have to worry about you breathing down my back every five minutes, and you don't have to worry about yelling every few minutes. It's easier for all of us."

"Alright you two, enough of the chit-chat. You're going to be late for your own graduation."

"True dat, let's go cuz I don't want to be late. Enough of the mushy stuff."

I grabbed my cap and gown off the arm of the couch, then we made our way out the door. I made sure to lock the door on our way out. When we made it outside, my parents lined us up to take pictures. Markel and I stood in the middle, Millian stood on the side of me, and Kitanya stood on the side of Markel. Two pictures in, Kitanya and Millian switched places. Afterwards, we were on our way. Me and the girls rode with Markel, and my parents rode in my father's car, right behind us.

CHAPTER 15

One Happy Family

Zya

Graduation night

$\mathcal{A}$fter graduation, we all went to eat at The Olive Garden in Milford. Millian's parents and younger sister were in attendance, along with me, Markel, my parents, and Kitanya. We were engulfed in deep conversation. We were all laughing and enjoying the moment, even my father and Markel were talking and enjoying each other's time. But, when I looked over at Kitanya, she was looking depressed as hell. She wasn't talking to anyone, and she kept looking down at her phone.

I didn't want to ask her what was wrong in front of everyone and have all eyes on her. I didn't want to make her feel uncomfortable. So instead, I excused myself and had Kitanya accompany me to the bathroom. When Kitanya and I made it to the bathroom, I pulled her over towards the row of sinks.

"What's going on, girl? I see you at the table, constantly checking your phone. Not to mention, you're looking all depressed and shit. What's wrong?"

"Nothing, I just thought that since today is graduation day, that my mother would call me and congratulate me or something. But, I guess getting high is more important than seeing your daughter graduate... I haven't seen her all day, nor have I heard from her; I'm kind of worried about her."

"Damn, KiKi... I'm sorry."

"It's all good, I'm proud of myself though. I accomplished a lot in these four years without my mother's help. She hasn't given a fuck about me for a very long time. I don't know why I thought she would start caring about me now. I almost feel stupid for worrying about her ass right now."

"Well, cheer up and don't worry too much about your moms, she's grown, she knows how to take care of herself. Besides, you still have me and Millian, and now Markel and my parents. If ever you have something on your mind and you want to talk... Take your pick; you have all of us."

"Thanks." We hugged, then made our way out of the bathroom and back to the table.

Instead of sitting at the table all quiet and worried about her mother, Kitanya put on a happy face and jumped into the conversations that were taking place. I knew she was putting up a façade in front of everyone else. I knew what she was truly feeling inside and the thoughts that were racing through her mind. Her heart was broken due to the lack of love and affection from her mother. I've never had the chance to experience the lack of love and security from my parents, the way Kitanya has. I feel bad for her; if there was anything I could do to change the way she lives—I would.

After dinner, we all went our separate ways. Millian went home with her parents; they said they would take Kitanya home. When we made it back home, Markel and I chilled with my parents for a few hours; afterwards, we went back home and made love for hours, until our bodies were drained of energy and we couldn't move. I figured at some point after separating from our parents, that Millian, Kitanya, and I would meet up and continue celebrating, since this day was special. But it was already nine thirty at night, and I haven't received a call from either one of them. So, after getting out of the shower, I grabbed my cell phone off the dresser.

Instead of texting them one by one, I decided to send out a group text to Kitanya and Millian. It read: *Hey my babes, is the night over, or are we gonna go hit the streets and continue this celebration?* At first, I thought I wasn't going to get a response, but then Millian replied back first.

Millz: Hey Boo, I'm down. Shit, a bitch need a drank. Just got into it with Vaughn.

Me: GTFOH, not the perfect couple...

Millz: Fuck u bihh! Tell u 'bout it later. How we doin' this?

Me: We gonna pick y'all up. KiKi, you down? Two minutes went by, yet Kitanya still hadn't responded back to the text message.

Me: Kitanya, what's good? You haven't been right all night; what's goin' on? You aight?

Still, she wasn't responding. Millian called me, and I answered on the very first ring,

"Hello."

"What's goin' on, what you mean KiKi ain't been right all night?"

"Girl, she was tripping over her mother not attending graduation. She seemed a little depressed; that's why I pulled her in the bathroom to talk. But she said she was good."

"Nah, she not even responding back to us. I think something is terribly wrong. You and Markel need to come scoop me up, so we can go check on babygirl."

"You right, be there in less than thirty minutes. Be ready."

"Aight, I will. Just hurry up. I'll keep tryna hit her up in the group text."

"Ok, be there soon." We disconnected the call, then I told Markel what was going on and told him he needed to get dressed.

We both rushed to put our clothes on. Markel was done first, since he already had sweat pants on. I peeped him swiftly walk over to the closet and grab his gun out the lock box on the top shelf. He tucked it in his hoodie pocket as I tied my sneakers, then he looked back at me. I stood up straight. "I'm ready." I grabbed my phone, then we silently rushed out the house and into the truck.

We were on our way to pick up Millian, when I heard my phone beep. I looked at my screen to see there was a message. I tapped on my screen to open the new text message. Kitanya was finally texting us back. When I read the message, it said: *Help me, he won't stop hitting me. Hiding in the bathroom... I quickly texted back.*

Me: *Who is there? KiKi, we're on our way now! Who is there?*

Millz: *Who are you talking about, Kitanya?*

KiKi: *Jeff! He hit my mother over the head when she tried to help me. She's not moving, and a lot of blood is coming from her head! HELP ME, PLEASE!*

We were pulling up to Millian's house, when we received that message from Kitanya.

Me: *Millz, come out!*

Seconds later, Millian was rushing out her house. She jumped in the truck and we were taking off up the block. Kitanya didn't live far. We should be able to make it to her in less than fifteen minutes. I turned to Markel and Millian.

"I think we should call the cops; this seems a lot more serious than what we should be handling. KiKi's mother needs an ambulance too."

Markel looked over at me for a brief second. "We can't call the cops. I got my gun on me."

"Well, put it in the glove compartment or something. KiKi's in trouble, and her mother needs an ambulance. I'm not about to let that lady die!"

"Aight, you right. Call the cops and have them meet us there," Markel said.

I did just that too. I called the police and told them what was going on. I told them exactly what Kitanya had told me, and I also let them know we were on our way there now to check on her. The operator told me not to go inside, because the situation was unknown and anything could happen.

I told her, "Then let it happen, because I'm not about to leave my best friend inside her house to get her ass whooped by her ex-boyfriend!"

Then I hung up on the bitch. I'd completed my goal of calling them and alerting them of the situation. Wasn't nothing about to stop me from going in that house to help Kitanya out of her current situation. Why in the hell was Jeff there anyways? They'd broken up over a week ago. She couldn't take his cheating ways and habit of being abusive to her. This was the first time Kitanya had ever asked for help, so I knew shit was serious.

We pulled up in front of Kitanya's house, and there wasn't one police car in sight. Markel was contemplating on bringing his gun with him, until I told him not to. I didn't want him getting into any trouble when the cops finally decided to pull up on us. We got out the truck and looked at Kitanya's house, there was not one light on.

I looked over at Millian. "Why the fuck is it so damn dark inside?"

"I don't know, but Kitanya ain't responding to my messages anymore. I think something happened."

"Tell her we're right outside; maybe she'll respond to that."

Millz: KiKi, we're here, comin' in now. Where u at?

We waited a few seconds for her to respond, but there was nothing. So, we decided to go inside. When we walked through the front door that was sitting wide open, I flipped the light switch on. The living room was a mess; everything was thrown all over the place. The couches were flipped over backwards, the table was turned over, papers and magazines were on the floor, and the TV screen was broken.

It looked like a brick or something heavy had been thrown through it. We walked further inside the house not making a sound, hoping to hear Kitanya. But as we walked deeper inside, we heard nothing in the one-level two-bedroom house, belonging to Kitanya and her mother. We walked down the hallway towards the kitchen, and that's when we saw Kitanya's mother Ms. Jenkins face down on the kitchen floor. She wasn't moving; it didn't even look like she was still breathing. I quickly tiptoed over to her and checked her pulse; thank God, she's still alive.

I was about to help her off the floor, when I heard a noise come from Kitanya's room. All of our attention was now on Kitanya's closed bedroom door. We heard another noise; this time it was the sound of someone banging against something. We rushed over to the door and tried to turn the handle to open it, but it was locked.

"KiKi, are you alright?" I yelled out.

She didn't respond, instead, we heard her scream out as if she were in pain. Millian and I moved out of the way, allowing Markel to kick the door open. After kicking the door three times, he finally got it open on the fourth try. The door swung open, and we all rushed in the room just in time to see Jeff holding Kitanya by her neck and ramming a knife into her stomach twice. Markel rushed over as Millian and I cried out for our friend. Markel grabbed Jeff and punched him in the back of his head, causing him to release Kitanya from his grip.

He still had the knife in his hand as Kitanya's body hit the floor, hard. Markel grabbed Jeff by his neck from behind, then grabbed the hand that held the knife and rammed him face first into the wall by the window. Jeff's face crashed into the wall hard, causing Jeff to instantly drop the knife on the floor. Both Jeff and Markel were fighting it out on one side of the room, while Millian and I rushed over to Kitanya's side.

"KiKi, open your eyes! Please, you gotta open your eyes, girl." She wasn't responding, and her breathing was shallow.

Millian was searching for something to stop the blood that was pouring out of Kitanya's stomach. Markel had finally knocked Jeff's ass the fuck out as police officers rushed through the house. Markel came and stood next to us as Millian screamed out, "*HELP US! HELP, WE'RE IN HERE!*" Tears were heavily falling from both our eyes as officers and paramedics rushed into the room. We moved out the way, so they could do their job.

"Where's the culprit?" officers asked as they began raising their guns towards Markel.

I stepped in front of him as we all pointed to the corner at Jeff. They rushed over and placed an unconscious Jeff in handcuffs. We were asked to exit the room, so we did. We walked out into the kitchen and saw that Ms. Jenkins was also receiving medical attention. I bet this shit will get her to quit using drugs and pay more attention to her daughter, dumb bitch. We walked outside, because with all the mess around the entire house, there was nowhere for us to stand where we wouldn't be in the way.

When we got outside, I realized Millian and I were covered in Kitanya's blood. I don't even remember how her blood got all over us. But, we had blood on our legs and hands. We were standing outside for about ten minutes, when an officer came out asking all types of questions about what had happened. We told the officer everything we knew about today. We showed the officer the text messages going back and forth between us as proof.

I even went on to fill the officer in about how Kitanya was acting earlier at dinner. He took note, and I took his name. When the paramedics finally rolled Kitanya out of the house, she was still unconscious as they put her in the ambulance. Millian rushed over to them and asked them what hospital they were bringing Kitanya to. When she found out, she rushed back over to me and Markel to let us know. They were taking her to Bridgeport Hospital, since it was the closet to Kitanya's house.

When the ambulance pulled off, so did we. We didn't bother to stick around and see what was going to happen with Ms. Jenkins. For what? She didn't give a fuck about Kitanya all these years, so why should anyone give a fuck about her?

CHAPTER 16

Embarrassed

KiKi

Two days later

What would you do, if you woke up in a place you weren't familiar with, while being in so much pain that you wanted to just jump out your own skin? Well, that's exactly how I was feeling right now. I looked around the room a couple times, before realizing I was laid up in the hospital. After laying here thinking about how I'd gotten here, I finally remembered what happened that night. The night of graduation, Jeff kept calling my phone, talking all kinds of shit to me after I'd gotten home. I hung up on him a few times and refused to answer anymore of his calls after that.

At dinner, I thought about my mother and how she was never there for me. I thought about her not coming to see me graduate, but was thankful to have Millian and Zya by my side. Even though Zya and I had gotten into that crazy ass fight, she still chose to be around for a dummy like me. I was surprised when she pulled me to the bathroom in the middle of dinner. I was so caught up in my own thoughts about my mother, I'd forgotten to mention the bullshit Jeff was putting me through. He was stalking my phone and threatening to beat my ass through text messages, if I didn't answer my phone to talk to him.

After I'd broken up with Jeff about two weeks prior to graduation for cheating and beating on me whenever he felt like it, I found out that I was pregnant by him. I haven't told anyone about my pregnancy—not Millian, not Jaz'Zyazia, and not Jeff. I wasn't sure what I planned to do about this baby growing inside of me, or what I was going to do about Jeff harassing me. But, for that moment, I chose to ignore his ass with hopes that he would just leave me the hell alone. That night, when Millian's parents dropped me off at home, I found my mother getting high in the living room with one of her fellow fiends. Once I started yelling at them, her little friend left the house without saying a word.

I went on to scream at my mother for not fixing herself up and coming down to see me graduate. I talked shit about her being the worst mother in the world and told her how much I hated her. I said, *"I can't stand you and your selfish ass ways, I hope you overdose and drop dead!"* She was so high, that all she did was nod in and out of consciousness. She didn't care for what I was saying to her. That's when I walked out the living room, heading towards my bedroom.

I got undressed and took a shower, thinking Millian and Zya would call a little later to go out. I felt they were more of a family to me than my own mother. They cared about me, more than my mother cared, so I wasn't about to slow up on the thought of leaving out this house. As I showered, I thought about all the far away colleges I'd applied to. I applied to UCONN, Harvard, Ohio State University, University of Southern California, Columbia University, and Princeton University, just to name a few. I was waiting to hear back from them, among other colleges.

I prayed like hell that I would get into any one of these colleges, so that I can get the hell away from my mother and Jeff. There was no way I was staying in Bridgeport. Especially, not after Jeff put me through hell. Waking up in the hospital in pain, with staples in my stomach and bandages covering my face and the back of my head, confirmed it for me. I was getting the hell out of this city. Millian and Zya walked through the door, and I quickly closed my eyes, pretending that I was asleep.

I didn't want to face them, and I didn't want them to see me like this either. When they made it to the side of the bed, Millian said, "Girl, bye! You not even sleep. We saw you close your eyes..." Damn, I was caught. I opened my eyes and looked up in Millian's bluish-green eyes; she almost looked like an angel to me.

"Are you alright? We thought you weren't gonna wake up; it's been like two whole days," Millian said.

"Two days?" I said. My voice sounded dry and low, as if I were whispering, but wasn't.

"Yeah, girl, you had us scared to death," Zya mentioned.

"Where's my mother?" I asked.

"They got her at Saint Vincent's Hospital. They're treating her for head trauma, due to taking a blow to the head by some type of heavy object. She's in a coma. My mother said they're also treating her for the large amount of drugs that was in her system. Jeff's ass is in jail; hopefully he'll be going away for a very long time," Zya explained.

"Yeah, hopefully… But my mom, is she really in a coma?"

"Yeah, she is… What happened to you that night?" Zya questioned.

"I don't know," I said, because I wasn't ready to talk about everything yet.

"Anyways, you should be getting out soon. My parents said you can stay with them in my old room. My father also said he'll take your case when it's time to go to court and face Jeff. He already spoke to the police officers and went to your house. They moved all your stuff out, so you don't have to worry about going back there."

"Thank him for me; I appreciate the help. But, how am I supposed to pay your father for his services?"

"Don't worry about it." I smiled at Zya, because I didn't know what else to say or do.

I wanted to ball up, cry, and hide my face, because I knew I looked hideous. I had two black eyes, the left one was swollen shut, a busted lip, and a bunch of noticeable bruises all over my body from Jeff kicking and punching on me. I was so embarrassed, and I deserved to be, after staying in a relationship with Jeff for so long. I didn't want to admit to my girls that I was in a fucked up relationship with a nigga that I was so far gone in love with, to the point I chose to stay with him. All of this was all my fault for not leaving sooner. I've dealt with Jeff beating on me all through high school, but when he started cheating…

That was something totally different; not to make it sound like getting your ass whooped by your man is better than anything, cuz it's not. He would bring these females around to treat me like shit. I'd got threatened, jumped, and got spit on plenty of times. Yes, the female that tried to fight Zya too, she was one of the many bitches Jeff cheated on me with. I didn't understand how he could treat these females with so much love and respect, but treat me like shit on the bottom of his sneaker. I won't say I deserved everything he was doing to me at the beginning…

But, I deserved everything I was getting, because I chose to stay with him for so long. But look what I got for leaving him… He choked me out, beat the shit out of me, and stabbed my ass. Did I deserve that too? I wonder if I lost my baby. Even if I didn't lose the baby, how would I get accepted into college with a child on the way? How would I be able to get through one year of college with a child? I feel so hopeless right now. I honestly feel like I don't deserve to live this life anymore.

The doctor walked in the room, breaking me out of my thoughts. She looked at Millian and Zya.

"Are you family?"

Millian replied, "No, we're friends, but we're the closest thing to being her family."

"Oh, that's nice, but since you're not family, I'm going to have to ask you to step out the room for a minute. I need to examine Miss Jenkins and discuss something with her in private."

"We'll be right out in the hallway, KiKi." I watched Millian and Zya walk out the room; I'm sure they were upset about having to leave.

Once they were out the room and the door was closed, the doctor started checking my vitals and my wounds. Once she was finishing up, she wrote everything down in a notepad that she carried in her lab coat. She placed the notepad back in her pocket, then looked down at me lying on the uncomfortable hospital bed, as I looked up at her waiting for her to speak.

"Miss Jenkins, I didn't know if you wanted your friends to know… But the baby is fine."

"So, I really am pregnant?"

"You didn't know?"

"I mean—I knew, I just wasn't 100 percent sure. Do you know how far along I am?"

"You're three months and one week pregnant. Do you have anyone to support you through this? Where are your parents?" I turned my head in the opposite direction to avoid her gaze.

I was too embarrassed to speak about my mother; she's a crack headed dope fiend. Why would I want to utter a word about that lady to anyone? And my father—I can't stand that man. He walked out on us a long time ago. I don't even know where he is, but I'm sure he started a new family by now. Why wouldn't he have? It's been over five years since he's been gone.

"Kitanya… Your parents, where are they? Do they not support your pregnancy, or do they not know? You're going to need some type of support from someone that can help you through this…"

I turned back to face her. "Look, my mom is on drugs, and my father walked out on us way before that. The only family I have is the friends you just kicked out of here. But, I haven't told them about this yet."

"What about the baby's father?"

"My baby's father is the one that did this to me, because I no longer wanted to be bothered with him. All he did was treat me like shit and beat on me. Four years of high school, that's how long we've been together, and that's how long I've endured the physical and mental abuse from him. When I left, he stalked me. He threatened me damn near every day, but then picks the night of my graduation to try and kill me. Do you know what he said to me right before he stabbed me twice in my stomach?"

"No, what did he say?"

"He said that he loved me and would never let me go until the day I died. He said, if he couldn't have me—nobody will. I begged for my life, while pleading for him to take me back. But he stabbed me anyways... I didn't even get to tell him about the baby."

"It's a good thing you didn't; him knowing about the baby would've probably made things worse."

"What's worse than this?"

She walked closer and placed her hand on my shoulder. "I'm sorry for everything that's happened to you, but you have to be strong for you and your baby. You've got to give it your all to try and live your life to the fullest. Do you have any plans for the future?"

"I plan to go to college far away from here, but I'm not sure if any colleges would accept a pregnant student."

"Don't think like that, they will. If not, it would be called discrimination. Stay positive, you'll get through it. How are you feeling mentally?"

"I'm fine, I just gotta get past all this craziness, and I'll be alright."

"Alright, I'm going to let your friends back in. If you need anything, push the call button and have the nurse page me."

"Thank you."

"No problem." She smiled as she exited the room.

Seconds after she left, Millian and Zya came walking back in the room. I still wasn't ready to tell them about this pregnancy, so I kept my mouth shut. When they asked what happened and what the doctor said to me, I just told them she checked my vitals and spoke to me about my wounds and whatnot. They accepted what I told them and changed the subject. They tried to crack jokes to lighten the mood, but my mood remained the same.

I felt like shit, no—I felt worse than that, but I managed to fake my way through the visit with painful smiles and laughter. When they left, I lay in this bed and cried myself to sleep. I felt pitiful; I didn't feel important enough. Not even to myself, but I knew I had to find a way to get through these depressing feelings for my baby, as well as myself. I was never like this before—weak as fuck and miserable. So, why was I being like this now? I just didn't understand it, this newfound weak side of me.

Maybe dealing with Jeff all these years had finally broke me down to this, whatever this was.

"Dear God, please help me gain enough strength to get through this. I've never asked you for anything, not even to bring my father back to me. But, I'm asking you—no, I'm begging you—to help me this one time. If not for me, then help me for my baby. Help me gain control of my life, so that

I can show my son or daughter how to be in control of their life as well. Please, give me strength to live!"

I found myself praying, even in my dreams. I haven't prayed since I was nine, and now I'm seventeen and pregnant. Ain't it funny how things tend to work out? It took me to get my ass beat by a nigga I thought loved me, for me to talk to God again. That's crazy, but I'll keep talking to him until he talks back and tells me what to do. Because right now, I'm lost and blinded by love...

CHAPTER 17

We Ride For Each Other

Millz

$\mathcal{A}$s we walked out the hospital from visiting Kitanya, so many thoughts were flowing through my head. I couldn't help but to think something was going on with her that she wasn't talking about. I've known Kitanya a little longer than I've known Jaz'Zyazia. So, I knew when something was off with her. Whatever it was, she was tryna keep that shit to herself, and I wasn't feeling that, at all. She was looking depressed, and I wanted to know what the cause of it all was.

I didn't like when my girls felt they had to keep shit to themselves and couldn't talk about what was bothering them. That's how a lot of shit got started before. But whatever was bothering Kitanya this time, I knew it was different. It had to be some serious shit. Zya looked over at me as I was deep in thought, tryna figure out what could be wrong with KiKi. We were standing in front of the hospital waiting for Markel to pull up on us, when she decided to say something.

"What's good with you, Millian? Why you got that crazy ass look on your face?"

"I'm just thinking 'bout, KiKi. Something don't seem right with her..."

"Yeah, I peeped it her mood. Something else is going on with her that she ain't speaking on. I think she just has a lot on her mind right now. Don't worry 'bout it though; when she's ready, she'll talk to us about it."

"You're right, but I don't feel right with just leaving her up there with a heavy mind and no one to talk to."

"What you tryna do?"

"Can we push our lil' bowling competition back a few hours? I really would like to talk to her."

"Yeah, just make sure you call Vaughn and let him know. We'll be home; if y'all need me, reach out."

"Aight, girl. Love you, Zya."

"Love you more, Millz. Tell KiKi, I love her too and to keep her head up, cuz we gon' ride with her until the gotdamn wheels fall off."

"Aight, I'll tell her. That'll make her day, evening, and night."

"If anything, I'll be back up here later."

I waited a few more minutes with Zya, until Markel pulled up. I watched as she got in the truck, then I watched them pull away from the hospital's entrance. Seconds later, I turned around and made my way back inside the building. I rode the elevator back up to KiKi's floor and made my way back to her room. When I walked back in Kitanya's room, I saw that she was lying with her face towards the window. Her chest was heaving up and down, as if she was lying there crying.

I walked over to the bottom of the bed and touched her foot gently over the covers.

"KiKi, are you alright?"

I felt her body jump a little, her face held a pain-filled expression as she bit down on her lip. I rushed over towards the top of the bed. "Oh shit, KiKi… I'm so-so sorry; I didn't mean to scare you like that!" I said with excitement in my tone.

"Mmm—M… I'm alright—I'm ok, don't worry about it. I thought you left; why did you come back?"

"I came back to check up on you, but damn… If you want me to leave, then I'll leave. You don't have to say it like you don't want me here."

"It's not even like that, Millian. Chill out, you just scared me that's all."

She wiped tears from her eyes and cheeks, like it was sweat running down or something. I watched as she put up a front, as a smile appeared across her face.

"Um, so, what's goin' on with you, KiKi?"

"What're you talkin' 'bout?"

"I sensed something was wrong when Zya and I were here the first time, and so did she. I told her to leave while I come back up to talk to you. So, here's your chance to come out and tell me, what got you all fucked up in the head like that. And don't be tryna tell me it's nothing, cuz I know you lying."

"I'm just goin' through some thangs, the end."

"The end my ass! Whatever it is you're goin' through, you don't have to go through it alone. That is the problem with you and Zya, y'all bitches like keeping shit to yourselves until the last minute. Ain't that what happened with this whole Jeff situation? You felt you shouldn't tell us, and look what happened."

"Millz, I'm really not in the mood to argue with you about my life and what's going on in it."

"I'm not either, I just came to talk; that's it. But if you don't want to get whatever it is you got stuck on ya' chest, off, then just say that... You don't have to come at me like that, because you feeling a certain way. I came to help, not cause you more trouble."

Kitanya didn't say anything; she just closed her eyes. So, I took that as my cue to leave. I didn't want to start no shit with her; that was far from being my intentions. I just wanted my girl to feel like she could come to me if ever she had anything on her mind.

"I'll just leave. You know my number, so use it whenever you ready to holla at me."

I turned and started towards the door. I wasn't tryna stand around feeling stupid for tryna help someone that didn't even want or need my help. I don't understand Kitanya. You would think she would want as much help as possible. Especially after going through all the shit she's been going through these last couple months. Who the fuck was I kidding? Kitanya has never been an easy person to talk to. But, she's always been open with expressing herself to every and any one that was in her space. Maybe Jeff had caused more damage to her mentally than he did physically, and I just didn't see it...

Or maybe, she was damaged completely, both mentally and physically, and I was just turning a blind eye to her situation altogether. Whatever the case may be, if she didn't care about her own situation, then why should I. I walked out the room and the entire building altogether, without expressing another word to her. My feelings were kind of hurt, but it wasn't something to dwell on for a long period of time. I'm sure I'll get over this shit in no time. Now off I go to meet up with Zya, Vaughn, and Markel, to get this bowling match on and popping. No need to keep my spirits down because of Kitanya and her issues.

When she's ready to talk, then that's what it'll be. Until then, I'm gonna smile and do me.

~VENOMOUS~

Zya

"Yaaasssss, bii-iitcch!! Y'all suck, we won!"

I was busy moving my hips from side to side and moving my arms in an up and down motion, doing my happy dance. Markel and I beat Millian and Vaughn by 40; they scored 320 adding up both their scores together, and Markel and I scored 360. The bet was, whoever loses would pay for dinner, and afterwards, the winners would settle for buying drinks.

"We woonn, weee won! Y'all losers ready to pay for dinner?"

"Bitch, shut the hell up. We got this, no shame here. Don't make no plans this weekend, cuz we want a fuckin' rematch. Cheating ass!"

I smiled, while still dancing in front of Millian. She looked mad as fuck, but it was all in fun and games.

"Blah-blah, you maaaddd! Ain't nobody cheat, girl."

Vaughn laughed, "Yeah right, you kept tryna distract us when it was our turn."

"It worked though, didn't it? Stop hating and let's go get something to eat. What can y'all afford, McDonald's on y'all?" I laughed.

"Fuck you, Zya. Yup, y'all deserve Mickey D's for all that bullshit you pulled. C'mon, let's get the fuck outta here, fools."

We turned in our bowling shoes and made our exit. Instead of going to McDonald's, we settled for the diner up the street. Once we got inside the diner, we found a booth right by the door. As soon as we sat down, a waitress came over and took our orders. We all ordered and went straight into an intense conversation about Kitanya.

"Nah, she was acting hella funny. She's really hiding something. I felt funny tryna help her out when she didn't want my help."

"You gotta remember, she's been through way more shit than the both of us put together. She just got stabbed up and beat the fuck up by her ex; she's not about to be wide the fuck open with us. Just let her come to us when she's ready—no pressure."

"Whateva, she needs to say something. Whatever she's holding onto is going to eat her ass up, if she don't talk 'bout it."

"Aight, let me ask you this… If Vaughn suddenly treated you like shit, which he wouldn't cuz I'll kill his ass. But, I'm just saying... If he did, then all of a sudden, he came to your crib and whooped your ass and put ya' moms in a coma and then stabbed you up, you gonna be open to speak on it?"

"Maybe not, but still…"

"Still what? You just said you wouldn't be open to talk about it. You act like this shit happened a month ago; this shit just popped off… Give her time to let that shit sink in. When she's ready, she'll let us know. For now, be understanding to her situation, shut up, and eat cha' food, dummy."

The waitress walked over and placed our food in front of us. I ordered cheesy spaghetti and fried chicken. Markel had shrimp over pasta in butter and garlic sauce. Vaughn and Millian had the same thing. The smell coming from all these plates was so damn intense,

I almost gagged while placing a fork full of spaghetti in my mouth. Everyone at the table peeped it, including Markel. I placed the fork back down on the plate without putting anything in my mouth.

"You good?" Markel questioned.

I pretended not to hear him as I placed the glass of water to my mouth and sipped the water. I thought I was good, so I picked the fork up and attempted to put the spaghetti in my mouth, again. But, as soon as I got the fork up to my mouth, I gagged again. I threw the fork in the plate—got up—and rushed off to the bathroom, leaving Markel at the table with Vaughn and Millian. I made it to the bathroom in no time and found myself bent over the toilet, throwing up everything I'd eaten throughout the day.

"Wha—what the fu—bllaaaah."

Millian appeared behind me in the bathroom, as I coughed up more throw-up into the toilet.

"Bllllaaah—blaahhh… FUCK!"

"Damn, you good? What's wrong with you, you sick or something?"

"BLAAHHH! Cough-cough—BBBLAAAAHH! Get me, some waterrr—bllaaahh!!"

Millian disappeared for a minute. I flushed the toilet then dropped down to my knees; I felt drained. Millian came with a glass of water, which I quickly grabbed out of her hand. I drank some of the water; holding some in my mouth, I gargled then spit it in the toilet. I repeated the same thing a few more times, then Millian helped me off the floor. I walked over to the sink, washed my hands, then splashed water over my face.

"Zya..."

I looked over at Millian as I grabbed a few pieces of paper tissue to dry my hands and face.

"What?"

"What the hell is wrong with you? Is you sick or not?"

"No, I don't think so. I been feeling fine all day."

"So, what's up with all this throwing up, then?"

"I don't know; maybe it was all the different smells."

"What? Smells? Bitch, don't tell me..." Her voice trailed off as I looked into her eyes, curious as fuck to know what the hell she was talking about.

"What?"

"You pregnant?" she quizzed.

"Pregnant? Bitch, is you crazy? How could I be pregnant and not know?"

"When was the last time you got ya' damn period?" I stood there dumbfounded; that was a good muthafuckin' question. When was the last time I had my period? "I don't even fuckin' know, shit..."

"I think you pregnant, Zya. You need to stop somewhere and get a pregnancy test. Do you think Markel noticed?"

"If you noticed, I'm sure he noticed that shit too." I shook my head from side to side, before my head fell downwards towards my chest.

Tears started flowing down my face, uncontrollably. I wasn't thinking about what Markel would say, or how he would feel if I were to find out that I was pregnant. I was thinking about what my parents would say. Especially my father; he's been hard on Markel since he found out about him. They just started getting along with each other for my sake. But, if I find out that I am with child, I'm sure my father would freak the fuck out, if he found out.

"How about you wipe ya' face so we can go back to the table. Just tell Markel you not feeling too good, and on the way home you need to stop by Walgreens or CVS to pick up some cold medicine. If he ask, tell him that you think you coming down with the flu or some shit believable. Simple ain't it? C'mon."

I wiped my face before walking out of the bathroom with Millian. If I told Markel that bullshit, I doubt that he would believe my ass. It didn't sound real at all, and I wasn't gonna throw it up in the air either. I decided to wait and go by myself, when I had the time. Right now, I didn't want to have everybody up in my business just yet. With all the excitement of graduating and the drama surrounding Kitanya, I wasn't even paying attention to the fact that I haven't had my period.

I was so far off track, I couldn't even think of the last time I had it. I didn't even want to think about being pregnant right now. I don't want to have a baby right now. I had plans on going to college this fall. If I'm pregnant, my plans to go to school were over. What am I gonna do? As we walked back to the table, Millian looked back at me.

"You good?" she whispered. I nodded my head in silence.

We made it back over to the table and sat down. Markel looked over at me.

"I had them put your food in a container. I didn't think you would want to eat after all dat."

"Thank you," I said as I looked down at the container of food sitting in front of me. "If y'all done, can we go? I'm not feeling too good; I need to lay my ass down."

"We good to go," Vaughn mentioned.

Soon after, we were heading out the door after leaving a tip and paying for the check at the register. Markel dropped Millian and Vaughn off first, then we headed home ourselves. I laid my seat back a little and closed my eyes, trying to focus on not throwing up all over Markel's truck. After about 20 minutes, I felt Markel's truck come to a complete stop. Seconds after coming to a stop, I heard the door open and close. I just continued to lay there with my eyes closed, trying to relax.

The truck was still running, so I figured he pulled into a gas station to refill his tank. I thought about getting out and getting a soda, but I didn't. I was too damn comfortable where I was, so I didn't bother to move. When I heard the door open and close once more, my eyes popped open. I looked over at Markel in time to see him place a white plastic Walgreens bag on my legs.

"What's this?" I questioned.

"That's for you, since you not feeling good."

"What is it, cold medicine?"

"Look inside and find out." He switched gears and pulled off, pulling out of the parking lot.

I thought about not looking in the bag, because I had so many different thoughts floating around in my head. But, I did; I looked in the bag and saw a Sprite soda, cold and flu medicine, and a pregnancy test. My eyes grew wide as I spotted the pregnancy test. I looked over at Markel as he continued to look forward at the road ahead. I couldn't say shit; I just turned away, closed the bag, and then closed my eyes until we made it to the house. When we got out the truck and in the house, I walked into the bathroom with the bag in hand, to get rid of this nasty taste in my mouth.

I placed the bag on the sink and grabbed my toothbrush and spread toothpaste across it. After placing it in the running water, I began brushing my teeth. The Walgreens bag hit the floor, and all its contents rolled out, including the pregnancy test. I watched the box slide a couple feet away from me.

"Fuck it, guess it's better to know than not know at all…"

I finished brushing my teeth, then I decided to take the pregnancy test to get the shit over and done with. I was confident that I wasn't pregnant, and was probably coming down with a stomach bug or cold. I pulled my pants and panties down as I sat on the toilet. I grabbed the pregnancy test off the floor, broke open the box, took the test out of the inner wrapper, and then proceeded to pee on the tip of the stick. When I was done, I sat the pregnancy test on the sink and wiped myself, flushed the toilet, and then got up and fixed my clothes. I washed my hands, then pulled my hair back into a low bun.

When I was done putting my hair up in a bun, I walked out the bathroom without looking down at the results of the test, nor did I move it off the sink. Instead, I picked up everything else and walked out the bathroom. I headed straight to the bedroom, got undressed, and lay down in the bed. I don't know where Markel was; I didn't bother looking for him either. I turned out the light, then got in bed. I lay there until I fell asleep, forgetting about the pregnancy test results and all the stress that was bound to take over my mind and body, if I knew the outcome.

CHAPTER 18

Good or Bad

Zya

The next day

I woke up to nothing but the sound of birds chirping outside the window, as a cool breeze blew through the curtains. I looked around to see no Markel. I sat up in bed, stretched, and as I turned to get out of bed, I noticed the test that I took yesterday evening was now sitting on the nightstand that sat on my side of the bed. Now, if this was some type of dream, I would think that it was a sign from God telling me to pay attention. But it wasn't; it was Markel telling me to look at the damn results, something I didn't want to do. But since it was here, I didn't really have a choice. I reached over and picked up the test off the nightstand; I looked down at the small window where the results awaited.

I saw two lines, confirming this unknown pregnancy that I feared since yesterday. I was shocked, because I had my doubts about being pregnant. But then again, I guess all the signs were there. I hadn't had my period, certain smells were too much for me, and now that I'm looking down at myself, I notice that I have put on a few extra pounds to my already thick body. How could I deny it any longer? Since I lost my virginity to Markel, we've been fucking like jackrabbits.

I lowered my head and closed my eyes, because I wasn't prepared for this long ass road ahead of me, with the heavy load I would have to carry upon my shoulders sooner than later. How the hell was I gonna tell my parents? That's the only thing that really bothered me; that and the fact that I may have to put off going back to school in the fall. Going to college may have to be one of my biggest sacrifices, because I won't be able to care for a child and go to school at the same damn time. Not to mention, Markel's life isn't one that I would want to raise a child in either. He's a fucking street nigga; I wasn't sure what he did in them streets.

I just know his ass was in those streets doing something, and that something had to be dealing with him hustling. What if whatever he was doing in the streets came back to bite him in the ass, and me and the baby ended up in danger over his street shit? Honestly, I really don't care what he does, as long as he don't bring that shit around me. But, it's not just about me anymore. It's now also about our unborn child…

I got up and walked out the room with the pregnancy test in my hand. I walked into the kitchen and tossed it in the garbage. I had no thoughts running through my head that were telling me to keep this baby. I just wasn't ready, not right now, and I don't think Markel is ready for all the baggage that would come with having a baby right now, either. He would have to walk away from all that shit he was doing in the streets, and I doubt he would be willing to do that. After throwing the test in the trash, I walked over to the cabinet and grabbed a tall plastic cup, then walked over to the refrigerator and poured me a cup of orange juice.

I walked out the kitchen and into the living room, to see Markel sitting on the sofa smoking a blunt, while watching *The Steve Wilkos Show*. I couldn't stand watching shit like this. I didn't understand the point of these shows, besides going on TV to make yourself look stupid. I sat on the opposite side of the sofa away from Markel, so that I could put my feet up. Markel glanced over at me, but didn't say anything. Once he turned back to face the TV, he got up and walked right out the front door. I didn't know what his problem was, but it's whatever.

I was unbothered by him getting up and walking out the house without speaking to me. He must have some type of attitude or issue towards me. So, since he wasn't tryna share what that was, I didn't care to allow it to linger in my head. Today was already starting out as a shitty day, which had me wishing I could lay back down and sleep the day away. I heard a ringing sound coming from the back room. I looked around, realizing I'd forgotten my phone in the bedroom. I got up and rushed to the room in time to answer the phone, before the caller decided to hang up. I hopped my ass on top of the bed, then quickly crawled to the other side of the bed and grabbed my phone off the nightstand.

"Hello."

"Aye, what you doing today?" I heard Millian's voice speaking loudly in my ear.

"Girl, it's way too early for you to be loud like that in my damn ear."

"Oh, my bad," she giggled. "Well, what are y'all doing today?"

"As far as I know, we ain't doing shit. Markel stepped out, not sure what he doing… Why you asking?"

"We're going to see that concert at Foxwood's; do y'all want to go?"

"Wait, slow the fuck down… What concert is at Foxwood's that I don't know about?"

"I think it's Mary J. Blige, Ginuwine, Dru Hill, Monica, and a few other good names that are supposed to be performing tonight. You gonna go?"

"Let me talk to Markel, then get back to you with an answer."

"You do that, but um… Did you get one of them things yet?"

"A test? Yeah, Markel got one on the way home last night."

"Did you take it? What did it say? You prego?"

"Yeah, I am…"

"You gonna keep it, right?"

"I don't know, probably not. Let me get back to you later, I'm tired. I'm gonna try to get some more sleep."

"Aight, talk to you later."

I disconnected the call without saying anything else to her. I hope she didn't think I hung up on her on purpose. Even if she did, I was too tired to even care. Instead of getting up, I lay my head on the pillow and closed my eyes. I allowed my body to relax so I could try to take a nap.

If I could sleep through the entire day, I would—but I can't, so I'm good with getting just a few hours of shut eye.

No matter how much I tried to relax and fall asleep, I couldn't. I kept thinking about this baby growing in my belly. I quickly sat up and grabbed my phone and dialed 4-1-1 to get the number for the Summit Abortion Clinic. I can't just sit around and do nothing; I gotta get this thing outta me. I was 18 and pregnant; that shit didn't sit right with me. I couldn't even get myself to say that shit out loud; it wouldn't even sound right.

I keep thinking about how irresponsible I've been.

"Why didn't I make Markel strap up all this time? I'm so fuckin' stupid," slipped my lips as soon as I opened my mouth.

"*Hello, 4-1-1, how may I help you?*" a female's voice said in my ear.

"Can I have the number to the Summit Clinic on Main Street? As a matter of fact, can you just connect me, please?"

"*Sure thing, please hold on while I connect your call.*"

As I was being connected to the clinic, I heard nothing but silence on the other end. Seconds later, I heard a ringing sound in my ear and then a voice.

"*Summit Clinic, this is Joanna speaking.*"

"My name is Jaz'Zyazia Robinson, I would like to make an appointment."

She asked me my date of birth and a few other questions to verify my age, name, and address. I provided her with all the information she was seeking.

"We have next Friday available at three thirty in the afternoon..."

"Do you have anything sooner than that?" I asked, I just wanted to get this shit over and done with.

"We have tomorrow morning at 10, is that good for you?"

"Yes, that would be fine. Thank you."

"You'll need to bring your medical card, social security card, and identification card or state driver's license with you. And, make sure you're at least 15 minutes early to register."

"Alight, thank you." After hanging up, I lay back down and fell asleep.

~VENOMOUS~

Three hours later

I woke up to Markel standing over me as I rubbed my eyes, trying to clear the crust out the corner of my eyes. When I finally got a clear look at him, I noticed he had the pregnancy test that I'd thrown away, in his hand. I got up out of bed without a word being exchanged, as I rolled my eyes and proceeded to make my way out of the bedroom towards the bathroom. As I made it towards the bottom of the bed, Markel grabbed my hand, stopping me from going any further.

"You just gon' walk off like dat, you not gon' say nothing to me?"

"Like what—what do you want me to say? Markel I'm pregnant, but I ain't keeping it? Is that what you want to hear?"

"You ain't keeping it? Wait, hold up..."

"Wait, hold nothing... I'm not keeping it. I already made an appointment to get rid of it tomorrow. There's nothing to talk about."

"Fuck you mean, ain't nothing to talk about, Zya? You just gon' kill my seed like dat without even talkin' to me 'bout it?"

"What is there to talk about? We had unprotected sex, I got pregnant, and now I'm having an abortion tomorrow. There! We talked, the end... I'm done on this subject. I got somewhere to be."

I pulled my arm away and walked off, leaving Markel in the bedroom standing by the bed, alone. I wasn't doing this with him. I wasn't about to have a moment of regret, where I was about to keep this baby just because he's the Daddy. Next thing you know, my life is fucked up, and then I'll be stuck with a baby and possibly pregnant with a second. No college education, no degrees, no future—nothing. Then, I would be forced to work at some fast food restaurant, or I'll have to become a stripper in some sleazy ass strip club.

That's not about to happen; I'm not about to go that route. Not now, or ever; I'm not about to have a baby and have my life be over, just like that. I grabbed my sneakers as I left out the room. I walked all the way to the front door then slipped my feet inside my sneakers. I didn't have my phone or keys as I walked out the front door, slamming the door behind me. I felt angry at myself, because I knew I couldn't blame Markel or anyone else for this. I could only blame myself for being suck a fuck up.

I rushed down the stairs to the first floor. When I swung the door open, I quickly noticed an all-black Lexus double parked in the middle of the street, looking out of place. Two dudes with long dreads were walking towards the sidewalk, raising guns up in my direction. My eyes grew wide with fear as shots rang out in my direction.

"AAAAHH!!"

I quickly backtracked into the hallway, slamming the door closed and dropping to the floor. Glass exploded over my head as I screamed out, my body was shaking, and my heart was beating fast.

"MAARR-KKEELLL!" I screamed for Markel, and when he didn't come right away, I started thinking the worst.

Shots continued to pierce through the door and the walls around me. More shots could be heard firing from above. I didn't know what to do; for a split second the gunplay stopped, but I didn't move. I was too scared to do anything, so I wasn't about to get up and run back up those stairs for fear of getting shot in my back. This right here was a clear indication of why I didn't want to have a baby right now. Anything could happen, and I could end up losing the baby or my own life.

I wanted to get up and rush next door to be with my parents, but they both were at work right now. At this point, I didn't want to be here anymore; it wasn't safe for me here. Markel rushed down the stairs, where I was still lying and crying on the floor, balled up in the fetal position.

"Zya, get up! C'mon, get up! I need to get you next door, hurry up!"

I slowly stood to my feet, my body noticeably shaking, as Markel slowly opened the door that was now hanging off the hinges. As he walked me outside, crowds of people stood around, looking at the two dead men lying face down on the ground in a pool of their own blood. They were dressed in red and green with green bandanas tied on their wrists.

"Oh, my—my goodness," I said in a shaky tone.

Markel tried his best to shield my face from seeing the two dead men lying on the ground, but I still saw it all. Markel walked me to the top of the stairs and handed me my keys and phone.

"Go inside, I'll call you later. I don't want you to be out here when the police get here. Don't mention anything to your parents about this, Zya."

I didn't say anything, I just silently shook my head as I turned around and walked in the house, after unlocking the door. I slammed the door shut and locked it, as my body slowly fell against the door and slid down to the floor. Tears began rolling down my face as fear completely took over my body. I felt overwhelmed with fear and anger; I felt weak. I couldn't control my emotions as I screamed out, asking God why'd this shit have to happen like this. I asked him for answers and begged him to stop putting so many obstacles in my path. I didn't understand it; what the fuck was going on? My thoughts were all over the place. I was so angry, but at the same time, I was also scared.

Were those men coming for Markel? Why and how did they know where he lived? If they were coming for Markel, why did they shoot at me instead? What the fuck is going on? There were so many questions forming in my head that I couldn't answer myself. Right now, Markel couldn't answer them for me either.

After sitting on the floor in front of the door crying, I got up and walked into the living room and sat down on the sofa. I didn't know what to do. Should I call my parents, or should I go back outside to see what's going on? I didn't know what I should do. I was way too scared to go back out the door right now, so I opted for walking over to the window and looking out. When I looked out the window, I saw Markel speaking to an officer.

He handed the officer what looked like two pieces of square papers. I couldn't really see from where I was standing in the window. People were still crowded around the bloody scene outside of Markel's house. Officers were walking around placing yellow markers around the house, where bullets lay on the ground. Officers were going in and out of Markel's house. I watched as he spoke to the officer for what seemed like forever.

When that one officer walked away, another came forward asking more questions. I was confused, because I didn't know what the fuck was going on. After a while, I walked back over to the sofa, lay down, and closed my eyes. I was exhausted after that ordeal; I fell right to sleep.

CHAPTER 19

Something Strange Is Goin' Down

Markel

Five minutes later...

"Officer, I'm tellin' you, I don't know these niggas! I've never seen them before in my fuckin' life!"

"Sir, why would some unknown men come to your house and let off over twenty shots at your front door? There has to be a reason; I'm sure you know them. Look harder!"

"I'm not gon' look again, when I done told you already, I DON'T KNOW THEM NIGGAS! I don't fuckin' know why these pussy ass niggas came to my house and sprayed up the place! Why don't you go over there and ask them yourself!"

"Sir, how do you expect me to do that? They're dead..."

"Yeah, you're a smart one..." I shook my head looking at this dumb ass cop. "Yo, when the person in charge finally shows up, I'll be upstairs in my apartment, smart guy."

I turned and walked away from this dumb ass cop and made my way upstairs, while tucking my gun in my pocket, along with my driver's license, permit, and license to carry a firearm. My front downstairs door was shredded with bullets and shotgun shells. I carefully walked past the officers and whatever evidence they were trying to collect, and made my way upstairs to my apartment. I passed the living room, where a few officers were collecting bullet casings and taking pictures. I walked into my bedroom and packed a bag, because I wasn't staying here tonight. I also packed up some of Zya's things to take next door for her, since I already knew she wasn't gonna want to be around me after this shit.

The truth is, I really didn't know them niggas that were lying dead on the pavement below. I had no clue why they would want to shoot up my place. I needed to find out who they were and what their beef was with me. I did a lot of shit, from hustling to robbing niggas on occasions, but I've never crossed no Jamaican niggas. I wasn't that crazy; I didn't have a death wish. The JBM (Jamaican Boy Mafia) was a small group of crazy Jamaican niggas straight from the island that were into all type of bullshit.

Compared to these young niggas, I was small change in this game. I hustled on a few blocks off Wood and Hazelwood Avenues, off in the cut out of a trap house right in the middle of the block. I had a second trap house not even two blocks away, closer to what I call *Crack Island*, in the middle of Wood Avenue. There sat a few bushes, trees, a gazebo, and a few benches, where the crackheads and dope fiends chilled, day and night. On one side of the block, there sat a brand new laundry mat where club Azur used to be, a Chinese restaurant, and a liquor store a few feet away from that. On the other side of Crack Island, there was a Mexican bar/social club, another laundry mat also ran by the Mexicans, and a small Mexican restaurant that was family owned.

There were a few Haitian niggas in the area that we weren't cool with, but other than that—shit was straight. As far as I knew, I didn't have anybody gunning for me. Since being with Zya, I've been real low-key. I've been stacking paper and coming home, not extra shit. So why would JBM be coming for me? When I was done packing bags, I started to walk back out towards the front of the house, until I ran into Det. Stacy Mack.

She stood 5'7, slim, with thick thighs and a fat ass. Her eyes are honey-brown just like her flawless skin tone, and her lips are thick and soft, like her skin. She's in her late twenties—early thirties. Yeah, I tapped that a few years back when I was just a youngin' coming up in the game. I met her outside of a club that I was too young to get into. She was standing around talking to a group of females, when I stepped to her.

Back then, I didn't know she was a cop. I stepped to her filled with confidence and ended up bagging her. That night, I lost my virginity and became a man. I rocked with her, until this one night I robbed this older nigga for his car and money. That was before I even knew how to handle a big body car, crashed that shit into three parked cars on the Ave, and then hit a telephone pole. She was the arresting officer on the scene; I was embarrassed, because not only was I being arrested by a bitch I was fucking... The bitch I was fucking ended up being a snack ass cop. Once I bonded out, we met up and got into a big argument about her being a cop and arresting me. I booted that bitch to the curb and went about my business and look, now she was standing in my house, looking me dead in my eyes like it was our first time meeting.

"Well, well, well, look who it is... How have you been Mr. Spencer?"

"Mack, tell me you're not the detective on this case..."

"Yup, it's my case. Care to share what's goin' on with an old friend?" she questioned as she walked away from me and into the living room. I walked in the living room following right behind her, stopping just a few feet in the entrance.

"I told those other two officers everything."

"Well, tell me, because I'm not them. You didn't talk to me, did you?"

I took a deep breath to calm my nerves, because I knew she was on some get back shit after so long.

"Niggas rolled up to my crib and shot the place up. They almost got my girl as she was leaving out the house, but instead she ducked back inside the hallway. They proceeded to light up the door, while aiming for her."

"Who did you piss off this time?"

"I don't know what you talkin' 'bout..."

"I'm sure you stole someone's car, or money, and now they want revenge on your ass. So, who was it?"

"Again, I don't know what the fuck you talkin' 'bout. You need to get outta whatever head space you're in that's making your thoughts drift back into the past, cuz I ain't on dat. My girl was almost killed; how 'bout you focus more on dat."

"Why do you have a gun, if nobody is coming for you?"

"I have a gun to protect myself, my girl, and my home. I ain't worried 'bout nothing else besides that. Look, if you not 'bouta ask questions about what happened, then you can leave."

"I see you're a bit hostile, sir. I'm gonna have to ask you to calm down, or I'll have to cuff you."

I looked at her like she was crazy, which she was.

"You not gon' stand in my house and treat me like a criminal, like I've done something wrong. You put cuffs on me, and I will slap a law suit on yo' ass, along with sexual harassment charges, Det. Mack. I'm gon' ask you one time to leave and go do your job, yo. Get out my house, and if you have any questions in the near future, have one of your officers call me and ask me over the phone."

She smiled as she walked past me towards the door. When she was only a few feet away from me, but standing towards the side of me, she turned and looked at the side of my face as I continued to look forward, to avoid making eye contact.

"Where's the girl? She's a witness to what happened. I am going to need to speak to her."

"That's not gon' happen. I'm not involving her. And knowing

you—you probably want to see her for reasons outside of this case. I don't have time for your drama and neither does she. You can send someone else to take her statement, cuz I ain't allowing you to go nowhere near her."

Stacy giggled as she made her way out the door. I don't know what the fuck she was laughing at. Shit, I ain't find nothing funny. This whole situation was fucked up in so many ways. The more I thought about this situation, the harder I tried to think of someone that would've wanted me dead. Still, I came up empty; I couldn't think of one single person that wanted me dead and gone.

~VENOMOUS~

Zya

Later that evening ...

I was awakened by the sound of the doorbell ringing and someone knocking on the front door. I got up, rubbing my eyes as I made my way to the front door. I tried my best to allow what happened earlier to evaporate from my mind. I looked through the peephole and saw Markel standing outside the door. At first, I thought about not opening the door for his ass, but then I decided to let him in. I unlocked the door, then swung it open.

As Markel made his way inside, I saw a female dressed in a white, button down, collar shirt and black khaki looking pants and a pair of black pumps, walking up the front steps towards me as I stood in the doorway. Her hair was pulled back into a long ponytail that hung past her shoulders. She wore a natural beige color lipstick on her lips and she looked to be about my height. She was beautiful with her honey-brown eyes and flawless skin tone. I peeped how she was walking towards me like she was sashaying down a small runway, like a model. Who was this lady and who was she tryna impress with her slow motion walking ass?

When she finally made it to the doorway, she stopped in front of me outside the door.

"Good evening, I'm Det. Stacy Mack. Are you Mr. Markel Spencer's girlfriend?"

I turned to look at Markel just in time to see him turn around to face the doorway with a surprised look on his face. He'd stopped seconds from entering the living room. I didn't say anything to Markel as I peeped the look on his face and turned back around to face the detective lady standing outside my door.

"Yes, I am…"

"Sorry, I didn't get your name…"

"Zya… Jaz'Zyazia is my name. How may I help you Detective?"

"I understand you were a witness to the shooting that took place next door… Can you tell me what happened?"

"Sure; I was leaving the house, as I opened the door I noticed the car and two men standing outside the gate. Soon as I opened the door, they didn't say a word to me. They just started letting off shots as I ran for cover back inside the hallway."

"So, once you saw them about to shoot, or was it before they started shooting, you ran for cover in the hallway? How did you manage to get the door closed?"

"What type of question is that? It was seconds before they started shooting."

"I just want to make sure I jot everything down correctly. So, are you sure it happened like that, or are you trying to cover anything up?"

"Why would I be covering anything up? What are you getting at, lady?" I peeped how she looked over at Markel, then redirected her attention back to me.

That shit was crazy, but instead of speaking on it, I decided to keep a mental note to speak on it later with Markel. This detective bitch was acting real strange for reasons unknown. It seemed like she was trying to accuse me of something—but what? I don't what it is that she's tryna do, either way it doesn't matter. She was starting to get on my nerves and piss me off.

"Do you know any of the men that were shooting at you?"

"Sorry, I didn't get a clear look at their faces, while they were pointing guns in my direction."

"Do you mind coming out to look at the bodies to do, oh-say-a line up?"

"You want me to do a lineup of two dead guys? Uh, I think I will have to pass on that. I'm not up for looking at no dead bodies, so no thanks."

She dug in her pocket and pulled out a card and handed it to me.

"You have any other information on what happened, or the suspects that attempted to kill you and your boyfriend, please give me a call."

"Yeah, right..." I watched her as she turned and walked back down the front stairs.

About a minute or two later, I closed the door. When I turned around, Markel had ducked off into the living room. I shook my head as I made my way into the living room where he was now sitting nervously on the sofa. I took a seat on the opposite side of the sofa; I didn't even bother to look in his direction.

"What the hell was that about, Markel?"

"What'chu mean? That's the detective on the case; she's a real dick. I asked if someone else could come talk to you instead, but that bitch real cocky and shit."

"If that's the detective on the case, why would you ask for someone else to come talk to me? Don't think I didn't peep how she looked at you..."

"Huh?"

"It was like, y'all knew each other on some personal shit or something. Not to mention, those dumb ass questions she asked me. She was comin' at me like I did something to her, not like no damn cop."

"Zya, you thinkin' too hard, dat's all. A lot has gon' down today; you need to just calm down and relax."

"Calm down and relax? How? Nigga, I was almost shot and killed today! How the hell am I supposed to just relax? See, this is why I'm not keeping this baby! I'm not!"

Just then, I heard the front door slam closed.

"Baby? What baby?" I heard my father's voice as he made his way into the living room.

My eyes popped wide open at the site of my father. "Daddy I— it's nothing..."

"It's nothing? You two are in here arguing over a baby, but it's nothing? Zya are you pregnant?"

"I, I—um, I..." I kept stuttering.

I didn't know how to answer my father's question. The more I looked into my father's eyes, reality started to set in. No matter how grown I may have been acting, I was only 17 and living with my boyfriend that I've only been dating for a few months; and now, I was pregnant with his child. This wasn't a good look, especially not in my father's eyes. Markel and I have been moving pretty damn fast. I knew my father was going to go ham on my ass, and my mother wasn't here to calm him down.

"Zya, I asked you a question… Are you pregnant?"

When I didn't answer, he turned to Markel. "You got my daughter pregnant?"

Markel looked from me to my father.

"Yeah, she's pregnant and wants to kill my baby. So, what, you gon' have her kill my seed too, all cuz you really don't like me?"

"Kill what? The baby? Why would she do that?"

He turned back to me, "Zya, you plan on having an abortion?"

I felt defeated; I had no words to speak. My head fell towards my chest as I shook my head in an up and down motion. I was pregnant and ashamed to admit to my father that I'd planned to get rid of the baby. "Ok, let's all calm down… Let's slow up for a minute. Zya, have a seat. And can someone tell me why there's a thousand police cars blocking the street and going in and out your house?"

My father looked from me to Markel; neither one of us spoke up. We both stayed quiet, because neither one of us knew what the fuck to say at this point. I quietly sat down on the sofa with tears in my eyes. My father didn't say another word, he just sat down in the chair as he unfastened his tie and released the two buttons on his suit jacket. I watched in silence as he lay his head back and closed his eyes. Usually, when he did that it was a sign of him being pissed the fuck off.

I was just praying that he didn't kick my ass up and down this house. We sat there for about an hour in silence, until the front door opened and closed. My father still didn't move from the position he was in, as he sat quietly in the chair with his head lying back. My mother came walking in the living room, looking tired as hell.

"Oh, hey Zya and Markel. What're you doing here? Why are there so many police officers outside? I couldn't even find a parking spot. I had to park all the way down by the corner and walk up the block."

She walked over and kissed my father on his cheek. Without moving, he opened his eyes to look up in my mother's face. She looked down at the disappointed expression he now wore on his face.

"Babe, what's wrong with you? Why you look like you done lost a major case today?"

"Your daughter got something she wants to tell you."

"Something like what?"

"Tell her, Zya," my father said in a stern tone.

"Mom, I'm pregnant."

"Pregnant? What do you mean, you're pregnant? Zya, you're not even 18 yet…"

"I know, Mom, I didn't mean to—" Markel cut me off as he stood to his feet.

"Y'all don't have to worry, she already made an appointment to get rid of the baby anyways. I gotta go; I gotta figure out why these cops

ain't leave my house yet. I'll bring the rest of Zya's things over tomorrow."
He started to leave, but my mother grabbed his arm, stopping him from
going anywhere.

"Wait one minute, Markel… What do you mean, **SHE** made an
appointment to get rid of it? You had nothing to do with her getting rid
of the baby that we are all just finding out about? And, what the hell are
you talking about, you gotta find out why these cops still ain't leave your
house? What the hell is going on?"

"Mrs. Robinson, I promised you when I first met you that I
wouldn't get Zya involved in nothing that I do. Up until this point, I kept
my word; I don't know what the hell is goin' on, but my house was shot
up earlier today and Zya…" He looked back at me as I looked up in his
direction, making eye contact with him.

I swore he told me not to tell my parents, so why is he telling
them? "I saw who did it!" I said, my tone full of excitement. I didn't want
my father to completely hate Markel's guts again, and I didn't want my
mother to think of him in any type of way, other than what she already
thought of him. She liked Markel a lot and thought he was a good dude.
I wanted her to keep thinking he was a good dude too.

"You saw the people who did it, you mean?"

"Yes, I came over here earlier to get something of mine out the
closet, and as I was leaving, I spotted two people standing outside a black
car with guns. Out of nowhere, they just started shooting up the house
while Markel was still upstairs."

"Well, who are they? Did they get away? Did they see you, are they
gonna come back?"

"No, Mrs. Robinson, they're not coming back. I shot and killed them both outside of my house."

"You have a gun?" she asked, sounding more amazed than shocked, or scared that the man her daughter was with carried a gun. My father's head popped up as he sat up in the chair.

"You own a gun? You gotta gun in the house you got my daughter staying at?"

"Yes, I do. I legally own a gun, Mr. Robinson. Despite how much you dislike me, I'm not all that bad. I am licensed to carry a firearm, and no, I don't walk the streets looking for trouble with a gun by my side."

"So, then why you got dudes shooting yo' shit up then?"

"I don't know."

"You don't know? How the fuck don't you know? You be in them streets; I'm sure you know what the fuck you do! So, how the fuck don't you know, when some niggas is coming for you? Especially, while my daughter— my now pregnant daughter—is around yo' ass?"

"Look, I'm sorry Mrs. Robinson. I don't know what happened, but I'll find out. I don't have nothing else to say on this. I don't know who those dudes were, but as I promised before, I won't have Zya around that mess. So, I'll bring the rest of her stuff back here as soon as I can. As for the baby, we both just found out about her being pregnant, but only she made the choice to get rid of it. I don't know why she wants ta' do it, but she already made an appointment. So, at this point, if she kills my baby, she kills this relationship. I gotta go."

I watched Markel walk out of the living room and out of the house. I was hurt by his words and by the look on my mother's face, so was she.

224

My father didn't care; as Markel walked out the house, he said, "Go, take yo' ass the fuck on then!" Then, my mother and I watched my father walk out the living room. Damn, what the fuck was I gonna do now?

CHAPTER 20

The Beginning of the End

Zya

*W*hat the fuck was I gonna do now? Yesterday was such a crazy fuckin' day; I was almost killed, my parents found out that I was pregnant, and I'd lost Markel all in one damn day. I wasn't able to sleep all night; I stayed up in my old room crying the entire night. My parents weren't upset about me being pregnant, they were more upset that I'd planned to abort it, rather than keep it. I ended up arguing with my mother about me keeping the baby, until I was tired of hearing her mouth.

She said, *"All this time, you've been hollering about being 18 and grown now. You've moved out the house and into your boyfriend's apartment and within months, you popup back over here, pregnant with his child. Without being the adult that you said you were, you chose by yourself to kill my grandchild. I would like to know, how is that being an adult? Adults don't kill their kids."*

I told her that I can't go to college pregnant, and she told me that I was sounding real stupid. She continued to throw crazy shit at me, saying,

"If you were so worried about going to college, then you wouldn't've gotten pregnant to begin with, and what makes you think a pregnant woman can't go to school? I had you and finished college, didn't I? Stop making excuses and be the adult you claimed to be! It's not like any of these school out here or anywhere else can reject you because you're having a baby."

Maybe she was right; maybe I didn't think any of this shit through. All I cared about was going to school, when I hadn't even made up my mind on if I was taking my ass to school anyways. At the end of the day, I felt like shit. My parents made sure I regretted making every decision I've made since meeting Markel. My father blamed Markel for our relationship falling apart, which really isn't the case. The only person he should be blaming is that baldheaded monkey looking bitch and himself, not Markel.

My father kept pushing the subject of how I kept pushing him away to be with Markel and my friends. He kept telling me how I stopped giving a fuck about him and wanting to spend time with him, to be with Markel. It just seemed like my father was jealous of the time I was spending with Markel. Whelp, all of that is over as of last night. Markel made it sound like he no longer wanted to have anything to do with me—especially if I go ahead with having the abortion. I was laying in my bed with swollen, blood shot, red eyes due to crying all night.

I tried calling Markel all night; I even texted him a few times but didn't get a response. Due to me not getting up out of my bed on time, I'd already missed my appointment and honestly, I didn't care. I had some soul searching to do. My mother made me a doctor's appointment so we could see exactly how far along I am into this pregnancy. She was trying hard to convince me not to get rid of my baby.

Yet, here I was, still lying in my bed looking pitiful over Markel leaving me. It was all my fault; why was I being such an asshole? With everything that had happened, I felt like having the abortion was the best thing to do. I also felt my parents wouldn't approve of the pregnancy anyways. Shit, who would've known I'd be wrong. It seemed like they cared about me being pregnant more than I did. "Ok, alright…"

I sat up and wiped my face, "Jaz'Zya, get ya' self together bitch. You can't let KiKi and Millz see you like this over no nigga. So what, you may love him, but he's not ya' nigga no more so get'cha act together." I repeated that shit to myself like three times, before throwing myself back in my bed and once again, allowing my tears to pour down from my eyelids, covering my cheeks.

I bet I look worse than Kitanya the first time she'd ever cried over Jeff, or Millz ever cried over Vaughn's ass. I was starting to regret ever allowing myself to be so open to falling in love. I gave up my good-good and now look at me, I was dickmatized for life. As my tears blessed my face, I picked up my phone to check and see if Markel texted me back.

"Nope, he didn't… WHAT THE FUCKKKK!" I screamed out as I kicked both my feet into the air, while swinging my arms.

I know I was looking crazy right now, but fuck it. I was feeling crazy as shit, so why not look the part too. I had one of Markel's friends, Boobie's girlfriend, Treece's number stored in my phone. I was thinking about calling her, but I didn't; I texted her instead.

Me: Hey Tree, u seen Kel?

Tree: Yeah, he wit' Boobie.

Tree: Been here since last night, was pissed. Shit good?

Me: Yeah, can u tell him to call me?

Tree: Got'chu

Me: Thanks, ttyl

I waited for five long minutes to see if Markel was gonna call me back, but he didn't. "AAAHHH!!" I screamed out.

My mother came busting in my room with Millian following right behind her.

"What the hell is going on in here, child? Why is you making all that noise in my house?"

I turned to look in my mother's direction, and that's when I saw Millian standing right by her side. They both looked at me with this disgusted look on their faces.

"Eww, girl, what in the world is up with you? You look terrible!" Millian said.

I looked away just as fast as I looked at them.

"She's been in here crying over Markel breaking up with her last night."

"Dang, why'd y'all break up for? Mrs. Robinson, what happened with them last night?"

"She's pregnant, and she wanted to get rid of it without talking to him about it first. Shit, she didn't even come to me or her father to speak about it… I don't blame him; if I wasn't her mother…"

"MA! GET OUT, PLEASE!"

"Child, you in my house; don't be yelling at me! You don't run shit over here... You moved out, remember?" I watched as my mother rolled her eyes and walked out my room and slammed the door for a more dramatic exit. She's too fuckin' much, for real.

"I knew it. I knew you were pregnant. But damn bitch, why you ain't reach out to nobody? That's fucked up. You that full of yourself?"

"Millz, please, don't start too. I don't have the energy for this shit right now."

"You don't look like you have the energy for anything. You look a hot fuckin' mess! Bitch, get cha' ass out the bed and brush ya' teeth."

I did just that. I got out of bed and slowly dragged myself to the bathroom to brush my teeth and wash my face. When I got back in my room, Millian sat me down at my desk and combed through my hair.

"We gotta do something with this mess on ya' head. Look, it's tangled and knotted up. What the hell did you do to your hair?"

"Nothing..."

"That's exactly my point; you ain't do shit to your hair. Now it's all tangled and shit; pull ya' self together Zya. You put this shit on ya' self."

"Yeah, some friend you are."

"I am ya' friend, that's why I'm giving it to you raw. You need to stop being so damn bossy and get ya' mind right. That baby don't just have one parent. There is a father and his name is Markel Spencer— remember him? You can't be tryna make decisions about important shit like that and not include him in it too. How'd you think he was gonna feel about that shit? Fuck, how'd you think anyone would feel?"

She popped me on the side of my head. "Bitch, don't be tryna kill my godchild like that! You not alone in this situation, shit! You and KiKi better get'cha shit together!"

"Kiki?" I twirled around in my seat.

"Oh, you thought you were really alone, huh? You and Kitanya are floating in that same lonely ass boat. The only difference is, you got people to help you and a baby father that loves you—she don't."

Now I was really feeling bad about making the fast decision to abort my baby. It was unfair to Markel, my parents, and myself to have made such a rash decision like that. After Millian was done combing through my hair, she pulled it up into a ponytail, then she applied makeup on my face. Since I didn't really like wearing makeup, she made it look natural, as if I had none on. I didn't complain, since you couldn't tell I had any on. She touched up my lips with some lip gloss and told me to put some clothes on.

"You need some fresh air in your life, we going to sit outside for a minute." Luckily, I still had clothes here, or I would've been assed-out. I got dressed in a black fitted shirt, black stretch-jeans, black socks, and slippers. All my sneakers were next door at Markel's place. I told Millian to come with me next door to get my sneakers. She agreed to come with me, so we left my parent's house and went next door.

CHAPTER 21

Can't Be Without Him

Zya

A week later...

The day had finally come for me to find out how far along I was in this pregnancy. My mother and I made it to the clinic almost two blocks up from her job in the Brooklawn medical building. We spent about three hours in that damn place; two of those hours were spent waiting in the waiting room for my name to be called. By the end of the appointment, I had found out that I was a months and three weeks pregnant. The doctor sent me down to the ground level to get lab work done at *Quest Labs*. Lord knows, I was scared to death of needles, but I had to do what I had to do.

After getting my lab work done, my mother and I went home. When we got home, I went straight up to my room because I was ready to go back to sleep. I hadn't heard from Markel since that night we spoke in his apartment. I was worried about him and hurt, due to not hearing from him not once since that night. I didn't want to do it, but of course with no choice, I'd moved back into my old room in my parent's house. I'd rather be living with Markel than here.

Kitanya was staying with us too and just like Millian said, Kitanya was also pregnant. She came out and told all of us when my father brung her home from the hospital. Lucky for her, we had a third room that my father used as a home office. The room was cleared out days before she'd arrived, and my parents went out and purchased a new full-sized bed for her. The other day, my mother took her out shopping to get a few things for her room. My father has been checking in with the doctors at Bridgeport Hospital to get regular updates on KiKi's mother.

She was still in a coma, but she wasn't doing good at all. If Kitanya's mother passes away, I think her temporary stay would become more permanent. I don't have a problem with that, but I'm sure my parents would. There would be two crying babies in a house of four occupants; just the thought of all four of us being here got it feeling overcrowded already. Good thing I'm about to start a new job at Jimmy's Bakery up Main Street going towards the mall. I was notified that I would be working part-time in the afternoons.

I had no plans on being in the house much. Kiki was about to be four months into her pregnancy and would have to prepare for her baby's arrival within the next five months. We all were excited about her baby coming. Especially Millz; she was excited to be having two Godchildren on the way, between me and KiKi. That's all she ever talks about. Kiki's belly was showing and for some reason, her baby was very active in her tummy.

The more I felt her baby move, the more I grew excited and looked forward to having my baby. When I was alone, I always seemed to end up depressed and feeling lonely without Markel being here with me. I often wondered what he was up to, or where he was. I wondered if he was happy, wherever he was. Sometimes, I wondered if he was seeing someone else while he was out there in them streets. I prayed he wasn't, but I felt God wasn't really listening to me anyways, so I pushed my thoughts to the back of my head.

I often found myself texting him about the baby every chance I got. When I went to the doctor and heard the baby's heartbeat for the first time, I recorded the sound and send it to him so he could hear too. I sent him updates on the baby and my health, so he would know everything was good with us. I didn't want him out there worrying about us the way I was sitting at home worrying about him. I don't think Markel understood how much I truly love him; I felt like I didn't matter to him much anymore. If he truly cared about me or the baby, he would be here, but he isn't.

I was so caught up in my own thoughts that I didn't hear someone knocking on my bedroom door.

"Come in," I said as I lay with my back facing the door.

"Aye, we 'bouta go to the mall; you wanna ride with us?"

"Nah, I'm good." I didn't bother turning around to look at Kitanya as she spoke to me.

"You alright?" she questioned.

"Yeah, I'm good."

Kitanya walked around my bed and stood in front of me. She looked down at me as I continued to lay with my eyes closed and tears covering my face. Kiki sat on the edge of the bed as she touched my arm.

"Zya, you don't have to pretend like everything is gravy. It's obvious shit ain't good; look at you…"

"Don't worry 'bout me, KiKi. I'm good, aight… Go to the mall and enjoy yourself."

"Stop tryna pretend to be so damn strong, Zya! You're not, and we all know you're not. Open your damn eyes and release those damn tears, if that's what is gonna make you feel a little better. Have you even heard from him yet?" I shook my head from side to side, giving her my silent answer. "Damn, that's crazy. Whelp, look, you need to get ya' ass up off the bed looking sad as fuck, and put your shoes on. I'm not about to allow you to lay here looking stupid over him. C'mon, get the fuck up out this bed! We going to the mall."

Maybe KiKi was right. I can't continue laying around being all depressed and shit. I got up and wiped my tears away. I fixed my hair then put my shoes on. I grabbed my jacket, my phone, my keys, and my lip gloss, and then headed downstairs with KiKi to see my mother and Millian standing by the front door waiting for us. Not long after getting downstairs, we left out the house, got in the car, and made our way to the mall.

When my mother pulled up in the parking lot of Trumbull Mall, it was packed. One thing I hated was being in the mall while there were like a million people up in there. I can't stand to be in the middle of big crowds of people. My mother got lucky and found a parking spot one lane away from the main entrance. After she parked and cut the ignition off, we got out the car and walked inside the building. There were a few people walking around by the entrance inside the mall; which wasn't bad, but as we walked further in the building and turned the corner and saw all those people, I sudden felt agitated.

There were just too many people in the building for my liking, but as bad as I wanted to turn and walk out, I couldn't. I sucked it up and carried my ass up the crowded corridor with Millian by my side, as we followed behind my mother and Kitanya. We made our way to the elevator; KiKi pressed the button, then we waited for the elevator to come down from the upper level. When it finally made it down and opened, we moved towards the side and waited for people to get off. Once the elevator was clear, we got in along with two other people and pressed the button for the second floor.

About three-to-four minutes later, we were stepping off the elevator. We took the right-turn off the elevator and headed towards the maternity store so KiKi could get whatever she was gonna get. I wasn't in the mood to hit the maternity store right now, so I asked Millian to come with me to the sneaker store. She agreed to walk with me, but before going in search of the nearest sneaker store, we stopped in Abercrombie and Fitch to see what they had. It didn't take long for us to walk through the store and walk right back out. I didn't see anything that I liked, so there was no reason to stay up in there wasting time.

Soon as we walked out the store, I heard a female calling my name. I looked around to see a female walking towards me with a smile on her face. I couldn't see who she was from the distance, but as she got closer I saw that it was Markel's sister, Kim.

"Hey Zya, what you doing in the mall?"

"Oh hey, I'm here with my mother and my girls." I pointed towards Millz, "This is one of my besties, Millian. Millian, this is Kim, Markel's sister."

They greeted each other by saying, *hello* to one another with a smile on their faces. Millian went on to say, "It's nice to meet you. I didn't know Markel had a sister. You both favor each other a lot though." Kim thanked her.

Minutes later, Treece came walking over.

"Hey Zya, how you been doin'? What'chu doin' up here?"

"Up here with my mother and my girls, just looking around."

"Kel up here too; you seen him yet?"

"No, didn't know he was here. I guess that's good to know, though."

"Oh, y'all still not talkin' yet?"

I shook my head, "Nah, not really."

"The way he talks 'bout chu', you would never know… He in the building though, him and Boobie just went over to Lids. You should run up on his ass and let him know what it is, shit."

"Nah, he good. I'm giving him his space; I'm not the clingy type."

"How's the baby?"

Kim looked from Treece to me, "Baby? You pregnant, Zya?"

"Yeah, the baby good. Doc said I'm almost two months in and the baby growing normal."

"Dang, I didn't even know you were pregnant. So, what's goin' on with you and my brother?"

"Ain't nothing, he just needs some time to handle some shit. So he says."

"He not denying the baby is he?"

"No, he not doin' nothing like that. We had our own issues, but he just needs time to handle his personal shit. I'm not worried about nothing. I'm sure he'll popup when he's ready. I can't worry about that; I have to worry about taking care of myself and the baby."

"I feel you. I'll have to see what's up with my brother though. He not telling me a lot about what's been goin' on with him lately, I see..." Kim said sounding disappointed.

"Girl, you know he don't get nobody but his niggas involved with what he doin' in them streets. You and Zya might as well not sweat whatever it is he doin'. Zya, like you said, worry 'bout you and the baby for now. Markel will come around when he done handling his shit. He hella crazy over you to not come back to you; you know what I mean... I heard 'bout what happened. He tryna see what's up with them niggas from that day. So far, he hasn't found out nothing. Those Jamaican niggas on the east always doing dumb shit. Kel don't got beef with them niggas, so I don't understand what's goin' on either."

"Well, what's he tryna do then?"

"I think he gonna go see the leader of the JBM this weekend; the nigga locked up in North Ave."

Kim looked between Treece and me with this perplexed look on her face.

"Wait, what the fuck is y'all talkin' 'bout? The leader of JBM? Y'all talkin' about, Demarion?"

"You know him?" Treece questioned.

"Ah, yeah, I fucks wit' that nigga. He got locked up on a gun charge almost two years ago, he 'bouta get out in another month. What happened?"

"A couple of his dudes shot up Kel's place and almost got Zya. Nobody knows why it happened, and Markel tryna get answers. Because of that, he left Zya alone to keep her out of the line of fiyah."

"Why he didn't say shit to me about it?" she questioned.

"You act like he knew you was fuckin' the leader of the damn Jamaican Boy Mafia. Bitch, get cha' mind right, fool."

"Yeah you right. Zya, I'm sorry 'bout that. I'll find out what's goin' on myself; don't worry about Markel. I'll send his ass to you for sure. Ain't no reason for y'all lovebirds to be apart like that. Congrats on the baby; I'm gonna be an auntie. I'm hella happy to know that, but mad I didn't hear it from my brother. That's kinda fucked up."

She started doing the happy dance, looking like a drunken ratchet. We started laughing at her. When she was done, she hugged me and rushed off, leaving Treece behind.

"She wild; let me go. I'll check you later Zya, nice meeting you Millian."

"Same here," Millian said as we watched Treece turn and walk off in search of Kim.

Millian and I continued on our journey to the sneaker store. We headed down to the first-level, to since I didn't find a sneaker store I liked on the second-level, I opted for one of my favorite sneaker stores in the entire mall, Finish Line. By the time my mother called my phone to see where we were, Millian and I were walking out of Finish Line with two bags each. I told my mother to meet me at Pretzel Time on the first-level. I didn't feel like going back up to the second-level to meet up with her. In fact, I was ready to leave the mall and made sure I voiced that to my mother. Millian and I had just finished paying for our stuff, when my mother and Kitanya walked up on us. We made our way out the building and went straight home, where I found myself climbing back in my bed until it was time for dinner.

CHAPTER 22

No Need for a Storm

Markel

An hour later...

"Mar, why the hell didn't you tell me ya' girl is pregnant?" I heard my sister say as we all piled into my truck.

"Huh? What'chu talkin' 'bout?"

"We ran into ya' girl in the mall and whelp, the conversation ended up goin' in that direction. You don't need details of what we were talkin' 'bout. Just know, it was said that homegirl pregnant with my niece or nephew. I'm feeling some kind of way, 'cause ya' ass didn't bother to mention that shit to me."

"My bad, I got shit on my mind right now. I was gon' tell you..."

"Yeah right, like you told me that JBM shot up your house not long ago too?"

"What I need to tell you dat' for? What dat' gotta do wit' you?"

Treece chimed in, "She fuck wit' that nigga you 'bouta go see."

I looked towards Treece in the back seat, because I swear I heard her saying my sister fuck wit' the nigga that had his goons shoot up my crib for no apparent reason.

"What'chu say?"

"She—" Kim cut in before Treece could finish.

"I go wit' Demarion, the leader of JBM. I'm sure there is some type of misunderstanding. He don't even know you to be sending niggas over to blaze ya' crib."

"You don't know dat' shit!" I spat back, feeling myself slowly growing angry.

"Whatever, just don't go up to the jail. I'll talk to him and find out myself. If you go up there, you gonna make that nigga send niggas after you for real, and this time they won't miss. So, please, do not take ya' ass up there. Now, can we go? Can we leave already, so you can drop me off?"

"Whatever, Kim… You better start choosing what nigga you gon' fuck wit' a little better. You always make bad choices in men."

"Shut the hell up and start the damn car! You got nerve to be talkin', when ya' ass ain't even with ya' pregnant girlfriend anymore. So, stop judging me for who I decide to be with."

"Yo, shut up!" I said, as I put the key in the ignition and started the truck, then left the mall after pulling out the parking spot.

I was tired of hearing my sister's big ass mouth. I can't stand when she starts nagging me over nothing. Whatever was goin' on with me and Zya, if anything, she should blame her lil' boyfriend for fuckin' my shit up. Why would I want Zya around me while niggas is gunning for me? Her being pregnant is what made it easy for me to push her away.

Besides, I don't understand why Kim is fuckin' wit' me for, when Zya clearly said she was having an abortion anyways. Since that day, I haven't called her nor have I opened any of the text messages she's been sending me. I figured she was begging me for money to help her get the abortion, and I wasn't having that. So, I've been avoiding her this entire time. Until she comes to me and lets me know she changed her mind, I have nothing to say to her. After leaving the mall, I dropped off my sister, then Boobie and Treece.

Once they got out the truck, I pulled off heading to my apartment to meet up with my landlord. I know Ms. Karen is gonna talk off my ear for what happened. But what can I do? That shit wasn't my fault. How the hell was I to know niggas were gunning for me? I know she gon' tell me to pack my shit and get the hell up outta the house, but I planned to move out anyways. I found a one-family, two-bedroom home right up the block.

So, I ain't worried 'bout getting evicted over some shit. I just don't wanna hear dis lady's mouth; I ain't for this shit today. When I finally pulled up in front of the house, Ms. Karen was nowhere to be found. After parking the truck, I got out and looked up at my house. The house was riddled with bullet holes from the first floor all the way up to the second floor in which I occupied, but haven't been staying at since that day. I thought about just going upstairs to wait for Ms. Karen to arrive, but chose not to.

Instead, I slowly walked over to Zya's house. I walked up the front stairs and stood outside the front door. I was tryna figure out if I should ring the doorbell or if I should just walk away. I chose to walk away and leave Zya alone. Soon as I turned around the door opened. I turned around to look to see who had opened the door. I was looking back in Mrs. Robinson's face. She looked to be on her way out the door.

I turned around to properly greet her, so it didn't look like I was tryna be rude.

"Hello, Mrs. Robinson, how you doin'?" She closed the door and took two steps in my direction.

"Well, well, well, look who it is… I'm doin' good, Mr. Spencer. How have you been?"

"I've been good."

"Well, you know my daughter hasn't been good. She's been sick over your ass. Why hasn't anyone heard from you all this time?"

"I've been tryna get myself together. Has she—" She cut me off.

"No, she hasn't gotten rid of the baby, if that's what you were about to ask. She's doing good too. Why don't you go inside and see for yourself. I have to go to work, but I'll walk you in. Let's go."

She didn't give me no choice, so I followed her inside the house.

"She's in her room; go right up." She pointed up the stairs.

"Thank you, Mrs. Robinson." I didn't say anything else, I just went upstairs in search of Zya's room.

When I made it to Zya's room, I took a deep breath as I knocked on the door and exhaled as I walked in her room. When I walked in, her room was dark and she was lying in the bed. I couldn't tell if she was asleep, because her back was towards the door. I walked in and closed the door, then made my way over around the bed. She was lying on her side with her eyes closed when I sat on the bed. She was snoring lightly, which was new.

She never snored before while lying beside me, so to hear her now was all new to me. I touched her shoulder. "Zya," I said in a low tone, not really tryna wake her up. "Zya," I said a second time. I felt her body move a little, then I noticed her arm reach over towards the nightstand and turn on the light. She looked up in my face without saying a word. "Hey, how you been?" I asked, because I was curious to know if she was doing better without me.

"I'm good; why are you here?"

"I was in the neighborhood and thought that I'd stop by to see you. I heard you ran into my sister in the mall."

"Yeah, I did and I heard you was up there too… Thought you were too busy to be out like that, but you were… Why haven't you answered any of my messages?"

"I thought…" I paused. "I don't know; I was avoiding the drama."

"What drama? You don't make no damn sense, Markel. You act like I was sending messages to your ass to start some shit with you or something. I was only sending you the baby's heartbeat, so you know I didn't have an abortion. I decided to keep it."

"Why?"

"What'chu mean, why? Because, I just decided to keep the baby. That's why, stupid."

"I'm moving out the apartment."

"Ok, so make sure you bring me my stuff."

"Why? You not moving wit' me?"

"It's not like you asked me to. Besides, I thought you broke up wit' me?"

I took another deep breath, because Zya was already making me mad. Why was she tryna be such a hard ass wit' me? I know, I fucked up by breaking it off with her. But, I had a good reason to do so. Now, she's tryna give me a hard time with asking all these questions.

"Just let me finish working some things out so I can do my thang, then I'll come back for you. Aight?"

"You sound crazy. You'll come back for me? So, you think I'm so fucked up in the head that I'll sit around waiting for you to walk ya' black ass back in my life? You sound like a fool."

"You ain't gon' wait for me? Aight, that's fine, then don't!" I didn't mean to raise my voice at her; that shit just happened.

I stood up and was about to walk away, but then I sat back down. This shit was going left and that's not where I was tryna take it.

"Zya, I ain't tryna get crazy wit' you, ma. I just came to tell you what I planned to do, so you don't think a nigga was tryna avoid you in any way. Shit just a lil' fucked up right now, aight. I'm not gon' say we 'bouta move in wit' each other again, then some crazy shit go down and you end up getting' hurt wit' my baby. I'm tryna avoid dat' shit from happening. Ya' moms would kill my ass if anything happened to you."

"Whateva, Markel. Do whateva it is you gotta do. I don't care."

I moved closer up the bed. "Come here."

"For what?"

"Just come here."

She sat up and leaned a little closer to me. I grabbed the back of her head and gently pulled her in closer. I placed my lips on hers and slid my tongue in her mouth, kissing her passionately to let her know how much I've been missing her. When I felt her kiss me back, it made me feel a lil' better. When Zya kissed me back, she let me know that I still had a chance to get her back, and that's what I planned to do.

I chilled with Zya for an hour until I received a call from my sister. She was telling me she'd talked to her dude on the phone about what went down. She claimed that he didn't know about the hit, and that he hadn't ordered any of his goons to make a move on me or my girl. She also told me dude wanted to meet when he was released. I ain't have a problem with that, because we still have a fuckin' problem. It was still his men that hit my house, so unless he handles his business and controls his peoples, this issue will never be resolved. It'll only get worse from here, and that's something I didn't want to happen. I had a baby on the way and a girl that I wanted, no, that I needed to live for.

After hanging up with my sister, I noticed Zya had an attitude. I didn't bother to ask her what the attitude was for, I just got up and left. I needed to go next door and see about Ms. Karen and get some of my stuff out the house.

"Yo', put something on and meet me out front in like twenty minutes."

"Why?" she questioned.

"Stop askin' all these questions and just be outside in twenty minutes, aight…"

"Whateva."

"Make sure you out there, Zya. Don't leave me out there waiting for nothing."

She just looked at me with this plain expression on her face. I didn't say nothing else. I left out the house and went next door. Before I could even step foot in the house, my landlady Ms. Karen was there putting all my stuff out on the curb.

"Yo', what the hell are you doin'?"

"What does it look like I'm doing, Mr. Spencer? This is unacceptable; look at my house! All these bullet holes all over the place! Do you know, I found three bullet casings on the side of the house and in the stairwell? I can't have you here; you gotta go! TODAY!"

"First off, you can't just kick me out in the street without giving me prior notice. If you're evicting me, you need to file papers through the court and have me served. Yo' ass is lookin' at a damn lawsuit! Put my shit back in the house, crazy bitch!"

"What did you call me?"

"You heard me! You been lookin' for some shit to hit me with for a long ass time. If you didn't want a black man living here, then yo' dumb, racist ass should've said that to begin wit'!"

"You— I-I don't know what you're talking about, Mr. Spencer…"

"Yeah, you do! You ain't gotta worry 'bout kicking me out; I'll move out! I already found a place. So, bring my shit back up to the second floor and take yo' dumb ass home where you belong, wit' yo' punk ass husband! Fuck wrong wit' chu' lady? Next time, use yo' mouth when you got some shit to say and not yo' actions. Yo' actions gon' get your scary ass smacked."

I walked right by her into the yard, leaving her outside to bring all my stuff back upstairs where she'd taken it from. This crazy ass lady is bugging; she thinks just 'cause her husband is a police officer that she could try to handle me. Yeah right, even his dumb ass gotta go by the law. This lady don't know shit about me, except the fact that I pay my rent on time and I give her no problems. If something breaks, I don't call her; I fix that shit myself. Now here she goes, coming around here starting shit over nothing.

I could slap this bitch with enough stacks of money for her to fix this trashy ass house up with no problem. This is exactly why my black ass is moving outta here. I knew that lady was gon' say some shit to me about the house getting shot up. It's fucked up that I'm getting the blame for it, but fuck it. It's whateva, I got bigger problems hanging on my shoulders to deal with. I'm gon' have to figure out who the fuck sent them niggas after me, if my sister's man didn't do it. I gotta figure out why someone would want to come at me to begin with.

TO BE CONTINUED...

Thank you for reading. Positive reviews are always appreciated!

ACKNOWLEDGEMENTS

To Porscha Sterling, Quiana Nicole, and the Royalty Queens & Kings: thank you for giving me the opportunity to share my talent and my work with you and the Royalty readers. Thanks for your continuous support throughout the time that I've had the honor to write on a label, a team full of beautiful Queens and handsome Kings. It's been an honor thus far to be able to be a part of such great people and read the fiyah between the pages of your work. Thank you so much. I hope to continue to grow and learn with all of you. Thank you, Queen Porscha, for the opportunity to be among some of the illest in the game.

To Queen Latisha Burns and the Touch of Class Publishing, thank you so much for helping me grow as a writer/author. Thank you for being my editor from day one; even if you weren't my editor now, I would still thank you from the bottom, top, and middle of my heart. I appreciate a lot. Thank you so much for working with me and dropping jewels on me in the past, present, and also in the future as my editor. You are most appreciated.

To my family, my daughter, Nyazia, my son, Nyqwon, my mother, Sarah, my sister, Virginia, my older brother, Sherrard Sr, and my younger brother, Kashaun: thank you for your support. Thank you for being around for me, when needed. To my mother, Sarah Baker, thank you for always pushing me to continue on when my heart fell out of love with my dream. To my father, Jose Colon R.I.H, thank you for touching my heart, even in heaven. Thank you for the years of encouraging me, while in body, spirit, and the heavens. I love and miss you so much!

To my fiancé, Ronald Morales, thank you for believing in me and my work. Thank you for having my back and wiping my tears through the many storms, writer's block, and uninspired moments throughout this journey. Thank you for giving me hope and encouraging me not to give up on myself, as well as my dreams. I love you with all my heart; thank you for pushing me to follow my dreams. Without a dream, there is no reality!

Join my mailing list and stay up-to-date on new releases, sneak peaks, & much more. Visit: http://authormzvenom.com

I would love to know what you think about my work. Also, be sure to leave a review on Amazon or Goodreads. Thank you for your continuous support!

REACH OUT TO MZ. VENOM

Follow Mz. Venom on Amazon: http://amzn.to/2AHIEPX

http://twitter.com/MzVenom_1

http://Instagram.com/mzvenom_1

Like my Facebook page: http://facebook.com/mzvenomink

http://plus.google.com/u/O/+MzVenom_1

https://www.wattpad.com/user/MsVenomous

BOOKS BY MZ. VENOM

You Can Keep Yo' Side Bitch

Unappreciated: Enough of No Love

Unappreciated 2: Enough of No Love

Remy & Cam: No Love Lost

Remy & Cam 2: No Love Lost

Remy & Cam 3: No Love Lost

Remy & Cam 4: Forever His Love

Sin & Lazia: By Any Means…

Sin & Lazia 2: By Any Means…

Sin & lazia 3: By Any Means…

All Out of Love: Where Do We Go from Here

She's Obsessed Wit' My Man

Looking for a publishing home?

Royalty Publishing House, Where the Royals reside, is accepting submissions for writers in the urban fiction genre. If you're interested, submit the first 3-4 chapters with your synopsis to submissions@royaltypublishinghouse.com.

Check out our website for more information: www.royaltypublishinghouse.com.

Text ROYALTY to 42828 to join our mailing list!

To submit a manuscript for our review, email us at submissions@royaltypublishinghouse.com

Text RPHCHRISTIAN to 22828 for our CHRISTIAN ROMANCE novels!

Text RPHROMANCE to 22828 for our INTERRACIAL ROMANCE novels!

Get LiT!

Download the LiT eReader app today and enjoy exclusive content, free books, and more

CPSIA information can be obtained
at www.ICGtesting.com
Printed in the USA
LVHW08s2329191018
594247LV00010B/139/P